KZRADOCK
THE ONION MAN
AND THE SPRING-FRESH METHUSELAH

KZRADOCK THE ONION MAN

AND THE SPRING-FRESH METHUSELAH

FROM THE NOTES OF DR. RENARD DE MONTPENSIER

LOUIS LEVY

TRANSLATED BY W. C. BAMBERGER

WAKEFIELD PRESS, CAMBRIDGE, MASSACHUSETTS

This translation © 2017 Wakefield Press

Wakefield Press, P.O. Box 425645, Cambridge, MA 02142

Originally published as *Menneskeløget Kzradock, den vaarfriske Methusalem: Af Dr. Renard Montpensiers Optegnelser*, 1910

This book was set in Garamond Premier Pro and Helvetica Neue Pro by Wakefield Press. Printed and bound by McNaughton & Gunn, Inc., in the United States of America.

ISBN: 978-1-939663-28-3

Available through D.A.P./Distributed Art Publishers
155 Sixth Avenue, 2nd Floor
New York, New York 10013
Tel: (212) 627-1999
Fax: (212) 627-9484

10   9   8   7   6   5   4   3   2   1

CONTENTS

Menneskeløget Kzradock, den vaarfriske Methusalem: Af Dr. Renard Montpensiers Optegnelser by Louis Levy first appeared in *Maaneds-Magasinet*, a Danish illustrated monthly in 1909, and was published in book form by Gyldendalske Boghandel, Nordisk Forlag A. S., Copenhagen, in 1910. It was translated by Hermann Kiy as *Die Menschenzwiebel Kzradock und der Frühlingsfrische Methusalem: Aus den Aufzeichnungen des Dr. Renard de Montpensier*, and published by Erich Reiss Verlag, Berlin, in 1912. This German translation of *Kzradock* was reissued by Klett-Cotta, Stuttgart, in 1986.

I

KZRADOCK THE ONION MAN

I

THE MEDIUM KZRADOCK IN HIS TRANCE STATE — AN
ENCASED MYSTERY — LADY FLORENCE — THE SHAGGY
HUMAN ANIMAL — THE ODD MEDIUM — KZRADOCK'S
LITANY — THROUGH THE HALL OF PAIN — BATTLE OF THE
EYES — THE RED-VIOLET SCAR

What will be related here is a dreadful and bloody mystery, one that is still not entirely understood by the author. A mystery the Parisian police themselves have not dared look into too deeply, even though the Chief of Police has the means at his disposal. Because he too knows the medium Kzradock, who at this moment lies in a trance state on my sofa, bound hand and foot, with a dagger in his hands. This is already the fourth séance. By the seventh everything should have become clear, according to the hypnotic order given him by Lady Florence on the chalk cliffs of Brighton. The solution to this terrible and unprecedented drama, which has set so many of America's and France's best pens in motion, slumbers in a consciousness which only dimly foresees how it will be used. Lady Florence, who must speak because silence is so immensely dangerous for her destiny, has encased her mystery within a mind, within a human soul. And there it has lain well hidden, much more so than it would have anywhere else. None of our other psychiatrists have understood what is wrong with this madman as he incessantly cries, "Bound hand and foot, with a knife in hand . . . so pale on a sofa, a green one!" When I began treating him he was on the verge of collapsing under the weight of the burden that he carried in his unconscious. Never had I seen two eyes so exhausted from a consuming fever, never two so violently shaking hands. It was as if these hands sought to get a grip on the incomprehensible; these fingers arched as in revulsion— as if trying to wash off blood . . . One hand had a ring with a huge stone. I had indeed noticed it repeatedly but not attached any importance to it. Then one evening it happened that I came to my patient just at the moment when he spoke of the ring. He had pulled the solid gold ring from his finger, held it in his hand, and stared at the huge opal that shone like a cat's eye. I have never seen such a bemused expression. It was as if he were simultaneously enjoying the sensuality of life and death, the feeling of a bliss of profundity, the awareness of a new form of life or annihilation. I stood next to him but he didn't see me. He moved the ring in and out in front of his eyes and murmured his usual litany to himself: "Bound hand and foot . . ." I saw how the stone gleamed like an eye, an eye with a green phosphorescence that bored into the mind so that one saw only the reflection there of the will of another being. This green opal-eye commanded; in a thousand tiny lights it issued a secret order. In a cat's eye tiny bubbles of light-waves lie hidden . . . and thus it was with the opal: it apparently transformed a part of the electric light which fell down from the chandelier in the ceiling of the lunatic's cell into human power, into that which we call vision. At that moment I already half understood the importance of this ring to Kzradock's destiny.

But I felt I must awaken him from this state! What could I do? I turned off the electric lights with the switch by the door, and we were suddenly in darkness. But in that moment, as the light died, I saw Kzradock's eyes light up in the dark, precisely as did the opal itself. As small as those two eyes were, they revealed an almost fathomless depth. I didn't have time to look more deeply before the light vanished again from Kzradock's eyes. I heard a cry and understood that my patient was falling to the floor. I reached out to grab hold of him, and in the darkness gripped an ice-cold hand . . . truly, as cold as ice . . . and this hand squeezed mine like a vice and dragged me down with him. I fell and realized that the way I had fallen I was now pinned beneath Kzradock's heavy body. And yet it was a good thing that we landed as we did: it was only because of that that I escaped Lady Florence's fate! Kzradock's face showed no emotion—he might as well have been a corpse— . . . But how he screamed! Leaves in the forest primeval would have turned over at this screaming; every terror and all depths of the night were in it.

I was not afraid, but nevertheless took all precautions, because I know the power of fear and darkness over a mind like that of my patient. He could turn into a wild, shaggy animal, drop to all fours, and pounce on me. Criminal nature, formed by the strange, sudden understanding of many generations of their situation, could burst out and turn his hands into steel hammers, his nails into claws, his entire self into a terrible, willful colossus who had to kill. I knew all this, have seen it often enough. I know that the faintest sound, the slightest ray of light can trigger such spontaneous outbursts. Therefore, I was cautious . . .

However, while I tried—without moving or groping—to find the pocket in which I had my Swiss knife with its many blades, I knew that Kzradock was not really insane! In a flash I understood him! He was the solution to a riddle . . . had been made insane because of that. Insanity had been breathed into him. Love or hate had driven his soul to abnormality. He was above all else a medium—a strange laborer in the world of spirits. He carried the burdens of others and so could not overcome his own. What was he thinking of at that moment? What went through his overburdened head? What had prompted those inhuman screams? Had he seen something, felt something, heard something? But who, nevertheless, can push his way into another's soul? It was not really the darkness of the cell that had caused him to scream, to lie on the floor and shout in wild, short siren wails. He had of course inhabited the darkness with images and visions—and this was the cause: that which his unconscious terrors had created.

While these thoughts rushed across my mind, I still continued calmly to consider (and I maintained a background of calm thought this entire time) the whereabouts of my knife!

And I finally remembered which pocket it must be in! I freed a hand enough that I could just reach the knife, but it was not possible for me to pull my hand back out.

We lay that way for a time. Then, in mid-scream, Kzradock suddenly grew quiet. But the silence lasted only a moment . . . Then he began to weep, to whimper like a child. The danger had passed . . . A crying man is not dangerous. So, I sought to untangle myself from him, to raise myself up and turn on the light.

A moment later he lay, groaning and sobbing, in my arms. He didn't understand what had happened to him, and begged me to have patience. Suddenly he cried, in a voice full of anxiety and hatred, "Where is the ring?"

I pointed to the floor, where the ring lay. He staggered over to pick it up. But as he was about to put it on his finger, he hesitated a moment. I thought to help him and said, "Give it to me, Kzradock!"

A blissfully happy expression illuminated his face, the happy expression of a child who is finally about to be completely understood. But I saw that at the same time a struggle had arisen in his soul. He leaned unsteadily toward me, as if he would give me the ring. But his hands apparently would not obey him. They trembled as before, and to my surprise I saw how his right hand suddenly grasped the ring and slid it quickly onto his left ring finger. And the big man with his low forehead and thick eyebrows stood before me moaning like a wounded animal.

With an effort of will that appeared superhuman, he finally stammered those words that I had so often heard from him, and which I had until then taken for words without any sound sense or reason: "Bound hand and foot, with a dagger in hand . . . so pale on a sofa, a green one!"

Now I understand you, Kzradock, you deeply sunken soul, so consumed by terrible powers . . .

And I went over to him, took his hands, and my eyes sought his. How deep they were, those eyes! And how large the pupils, how unsteady his gaze. I took him by the arm, and as I led him to the door, I felt a shiver of pleasure go through him like a gentle wave. When I remained standing at the door a moment, I felt a feeble handclasp. Kzradock, of course. This pressure meant, "Lead me further, for God's sake!" I had expected it, and I paused at the threshold while I considered what would happen now. A shiver ran through me . . . And then I opened the door.

We went into the long hall, the immense corridor onto which all the rooms in this old Parisian insane asylum opened. How many terrors of madness could this corridor tell! It is a meeting place for terror and its martyrs. It is never quiet here. From one cell comes the sound of screaming and squealing, from another cursing and singing, from a third monotonous howling without end. Out of the distance, from the outlying corners of the corridor, sudden groans ring out, then a noise as if a head were being pounded against a door, and following that, the strange and sluggish sounds of steps and pointless sawing sounds which no one understands . . .

The asylum was housed within an old, decaying structure from the time of Ludwig XIII, at the foot of the southern slope of the neighborhood of the Pantheon, near the Rue Monge. In this huge house, which on the outside looks as if it belongs in some distant century, everything is dark and antiquated. But the long corridor is well known across the entire district. Only a few have seen it, but everyone talks about it. Ask anyone in this overpopulated part of Paris about the Hall of Pain, and they will direct you to this building.

I escorted Kzradock down the corridor. Arm in arm we went, like two wild dreamers. What he was thinking, I couldn't say. For my part, I thought about this curious patient who walked with me, and about his riddle that

I hoped to solve. Moving down the Hall of Pain, I felt I was approaching a scientific triumph. I felt it, a fixed, formulated hunch in my mind, and my heart beat faster in anticipation. I was silent and squeezed Kzradock's arm. He must not now—whatever might happen—escape from me. My future depended on the actions we took; as his doctor I was bound to him. Only as his doctor? I already had in my mind that he would also be a part of my future in some other way. I increased my pace, with a feeling of pride and curiosity, of hope and fear.

When we reached the end of the corridor, Kzradock paused a moment to stand before the barred window. He gazed out at Paris, which lay far below him in the twilight. But he didn't appear to be studying the city; he was looking at something else. I tried to find out what interested him there on the neighborhood roofs, some of which lay beneath the window, and I commented on a large black cat, a sinister, long-haired beast with movements full of half-tamed wildness. The animal turned his eyes on us, and the sight reminded me of the scene that had just transpired in Kzradock's cell. He must have felt something similar, because he suddenly turned his cold, hard, penetrating gaze to my eyes.

Then I understood that a struggle was in store, that there was still something in him I had to overcome.

My gaze held his, and I tried to penetrate behind it, and sought to repel the power his eyes put into the struggle between us. The twilight helped me, as his gaze was unable to lock securely onto mine because my eyes were half in shadow . . . and suddenly I was there, completely inside him, behind his defiance and his hatred. Then his eyes became as submissive as a dog's, and he closed them for a second . . . in what appeared to be a show of gratitude . . . Then, begging, he began again to murmur the same old litany, those specifically Kzradock-esque words which will echo so dreadfully in my ears for all time . . .

Now his wish would finally be fulfilled! We took the squeaky stairs upward, and then we stood in my room. When he saw my green sofa it was as if he were transformed. He smiled and laughed and began to dance with light jumps. Talkative now, he ran to the instrument cabinet, where he showed a rush of pleasure at the sight of the many shining, sharp knives.

I approached him.

I took him by the shoulder and led him to the sofa. He was quite docile now, and put both of his hands on the green cloth, let them glide over it as if caressing the cloth. Suddenly he threw himself down on the sofa, his hands covering his face . . . I opened a cabinet in which, I remembered, I kept a pair of bandages that had earlier been used for a young girl with a hip complaint. I took the bandages out of the cabinet.

Kzradock had stretched out his legs, and slowly took his hands away from his face. He lay there quietly, breathing steadily as if in deep thought. I had never seen him so calm. He lay there like the portrait of his own soul at rest.

And when at this moment I think back to the hyper-nervous anxiety which overtook me at the contemplation of his face, I almost understand the mystical power with which the soul is endowed when it either concentrates or discharges its power. I confess that I—a doctor of mental illness—have respect for the soul. At times I wholeheartedly love and admire it. However, most of the time I hate it like an enemy—an enemy who is always ready to take its victim by surprise. If worse comes to worst, however, then I doubt its existence. How terrible, how pointless! I speak of the soul, of its will and its strength, and then perhaps it doesn't exist at all, rather is only an illusion, an empty hallucination of the intellect. I fear the soul, and perhaps it is this fear that summons up my gigantic adversary and lends it form. My struggle with Kzradock, as it must develop with the passage of time, is like the struggle with the soul. Kzradock or I must triumph—either I gain the upper hand over his insanity, or he gains it over me. Oh, Lady Florence, the threads of life are spun strangely! Forgive me, lovely, unmet lady, for calling your name. Your fever has entered my blood, your will has awakened my opposition and spurred it on. Because you are like the soul, Lady Florence, like the unknown, the great feminine X of man! Do you desire my defeat? Alas, if I am victorious, you are defeated . . .

I said nothing to Kzradock. But with steady, determined movements I wrapped his legs and bound them together. (It surprised me at that moment that I felt virtually no calf muscles; it had obviously been a long time since he had had any exercise. And this weak calf muscle also showed me how weak his will was!) Then I seized his hands. He offered no resistance, and I tied them firmly.

The dagger was still lacking. I went to look among my instruments for a dagger. Of course there was none. But it occurred to me that once in Cairo I had bought an old Egyptian dagger from a one-eyed Jew. Where, however, had I put it? I looked in vain for a long time. Finally, I had the thought that perhaps I had stuck it in a book in my book cabinet. And it actually was there, stuck in the Bible as a convenient bookmark. I took the Bible from the cabinet; and the dagger fell jangling to the floor, when the book opened at the place where it had lain.

I left the book behind, took the heavy bronze dagger over to the sofa and stuck its handle between Kzradock's hands. He didn't stir. But he went pale as the cold metal touched his hands . . . Even in the ash-gray light of dusk I saw this. On his pale forehead a red-violet scar emerged, a terrible scar that extended up past his hairline.

I stood leaning over him. He lay as still as a dead man. Minutes passed.

And suddenly . . . suddenly he began to murmur something, at first quietly . . . single words only . . . then more loudly . . . and coherently. I leaned close to his mouth to listen . . . But what was this? . . . Was what he was saying true? . . . Unbelievable! . . . Inconceivable!

Could a human brain bear such thoughts? Oh, God! . . . Hideous! . . . I heard, nevertheless; I heard, I heard . . .

II

THE FIRST SÉANCE — INTO THE ABYSS OF REASON —
KZRADOCK THE ONION MAN — THE TWO CORPSES —
THREE HUNDRED FATHOMS OF WATER — THE YELLOW
PUMA — LADY FLORENCE

———————

I will relate the incidents of the first séance calmly, exercising self-control over the turmoil I feel in my soul. Still, everyone will surely understand my excitement as the curtain suddenly rose on this drama, one the Parisian Police and the American detective magazines have occupied themselves with at such length. I had succeeded in reaching the unreachable, but would I be able to finish the work I had begun? I stood in my room, where the bluish smoke of my afternoon cigar still lingered, and there on my sofa lay Kzradock, so pale, bound hand and foot, and with the handle of the Egyptian dagger between his palms. He was a picture of the destruction of the will, the symbol of dependence on an apparently insane reality. He obeyed hidden forces and was caught within the gears of the unknown. I can calmly write that now, but at that moment I felt only terror, tearing, icy terror that was about to make me myself a victim of the trance state. What were these terrible and incomprehensible things of which Kzradock murmured, things that nearly froze the mixture of my blood, while currents of sympathy crawled along my nerves? What was the secret in Kzradock's soul that sought to free itself, and which now, like a kind of exhalation of the soul, seethed from his mouth?

This was incredibility itself.

It was the incredible and the callow, wrapped in a crime, cruel and bloody and at the same time so tangled, so inextricably wrapped in blazing hatred, in consuming vengeance! And yet, all of this also showed an inexpressible beauty and loveliness. So, right from the beginning, I came to know Kzradock's worldview as such a mixture of all matters . . .

But, I have forgotten one thing. Something, perhaps, essential.

Kzradock's trance was of an unusual kind, in that he reached the state of unconsciousness without swaying, and without any intermediate stages. He longed with his entire soul for the solution to his own riddle. And it was at this moment that he gave in to a kind of spiritual law of gravity, in which he let go of reality and threw himself into the abyss of judgment . . .

"Deliver me!" he murmured. "Deliver me from my crimes . . . from all of them . . . from those I have committed, and those I only wish to commit. Great God, is there no deliverance? I say prayers to the heavenly powers . . . they want the great hands of the doctors to be bound, they want the dreadful trail of blood on the wallpaper washed away . . . they want . . .

"But still I see nothing clearly. Everything breaks into pieces when I try to hold it in place. What is that; what do I hear? Is it the wind? Oh, the cool wind . . . does it still roar around the unhappy corner by St. Augustin? She stood there then; where is she now? She, who holds all threads in her hand? I am lost, a thousand-fold and for all eternity I am lost, if those threads should break. Then I will be done for . . ."

Here Kzradock was silent for a moment. Then he added, "Am I lying under a bell jar from which the air has been pumped out?"

He attempted to lift his head, but immediately let it drop back on the green sofa.

"Quiet! Don't whisper anything into my ear. I am no longer a man. I lie enclosed in the web of my actions like an embryo. Give me my senses, Lady Florence, give me back my five senses . . . No, not seven! Where did this terrible number come from? Did you give me seven commands to speak . . . to return seven times to the world around us? And when I have obeyed this seven times— then what?

"What do you want from me?

"Tell me . . . listen to me . . . Why do you want me to talk? Because you also are weak . . . Or why?

"Did you foresee that I would have to obey you at this moment? The time for your design has come. Do you believe that it is approaching? See, I have found my place: this green sofa! The dagger is in my hands. Your design comes to pass! Oh, if I could free my hands, if I could break these bonds, I would never, never betray you. Yes, I wish it . . . Give me freedom, wretched one . . .

"I cannot, Lady Florence . . . you yourself have bound me. You compelled it. You have always kept yourself untraceable. And with good reason! The American detective is so narrow-minded . . . Who understands your rich soul? Who has grasped the invisible line, gripped the threads in your net? Fire consumes . . . and they burned everything on your funeral pyre, nailed the facts to the cross! They relied blindly on your intelligence. And what did you teach them? Tell me, answer quickly . . . conceal nothing . . . I beg you!

"Lady Florence, I have always thought only of your black hair. And, nevertheless, you know that I understand everything. That is why you have enchanted me . . . turned me into a plant . . . an onion . . . a body with living seeds and energies . . ."

Kzradock took a deep breath, and his hands, which still held the dagger, shook. But he clenched them so tightly around the metal that his knuckles turned completely white. And he continued.

"What did I tell you? That a person is not an animal? Rather, a plant . . . a germinating plant . . . a blossoming vegetable: I swear it! In your eyes have I not completely shot down the idea that there is an animal in people? Only . . . as a gift for your black hair and your eyes so full of lovely tears . . . I proclaimed the lesson of the plant in every living person. Oh, how you mocked me, even as you agreed! . . . You have lain me here as a victim of my own lesson . . . Did you imagine this when we spoke about laying the foundation-stone for a new humanity? Lady Florence, when I gave you everything, you took everything. The only thing you couldn't steal was the seed in me. It still lives behind the wilted onionskins.

"Am I confessing this only because you want me to?

"I obey, Lady Florence! We must obey the laws of germination! What do you want now, you who own my will?

"I know, I know . . . you want me to reveal the facts . . . You want to hear everything that happened the night of the third and fourth of May in the rue Vaugirard in Paris. No, not quite everything . . . Just everything the police discovered the next morning when they crowded into the studio in the rue Vaugirard and discovered Alice and Yvonne lying outstretched on the floor. I will tell you, I will tell you . . . First, let me catch my breath!"

Kzradock heaved his upper body so violently then that the dagger nearly slipped out of his hands. But I quickly put it back. And with my handkerchief I wiped the sweat off Kzradock's brow. His pulse at his temple at this moment was 120 beats per minute. He didn't notice when my hands touched his face. I pushed his eyelids completely back from his eyeballs without any noticeable reaction. Then he went on with his long soliloquy.

"So quiet . . . now I see it . . . the image, the reality. There lies Alice, dead on the floor in a pool of blood, with a knife wound on her neck. Yvonne, however, is still in the process of bleeding to death. The stream of blood runs under her back and is soaked up by her blond hair, as if rising from fine roots. Hideous! The paleness of the two faces, the half-open mouths, the staring eyes with their look of decay! The long nightdresses torn and slashed, smeared with blood. Oh, God! These two who had loved each other so . . . these two sisters and friends, who together had been ordained before the altar of music! Now their blood runs together in a large pool that soaks into the carpet. And the carpet is so red that you can hardly tell what is blood and what is carpet.

"And I? I arrive at the scene with the police inspector, Mr. Vernet. He has a large file under his arm. This small man with the dark complexion still stands on the threshold. How his eyes widen at the sight! Oh, how brutally cold it is, although it is early spring. What is that sound? It's the rain, falling against the high windows of the studio, unrelenting, alarming, a continuous racket. Drops fall on my head! . . . I am close to fainting! The close air of the studio, the reek of blood, and yet another smell that for a moment I don't recognize . . . the two unfortunate women in their bloody nightdresses . . . and the medical bag of the doctor who has also been called in, with his gleaming instruments . . .

"Look, now he bends over Yvonne, gently turning her beautiful head, so that her face is freed from her bloody hair . . . What is this? She also has a wound on her neck . . . as if from claws.

"And what are those tracks on the carpet and the floor? Bloody tracks of huge cat paws . . . And what sort of animal is this that lies curled up under the divan, its bloody face turned toward the entryway? . . . I see it and my blood freezes. And at that moment I believed I understood everything . . . and what did I understand? It was Bayle, the puma! Your beloved puma, Lady Florence! Here I saw again, to my horror, the yellow predator you had brought from South America, which had disappeared into Paris without a trace . . . Bayle, the American lion—your comrade, as you called him. With you, he was always friendly, loyal and as gentle as a child. For you, Lady Florence, he was as obedient as a man. You could do with him as you pleased; he followed you everywhere like a big lazy dog. How often I saw how your supple fingers stroked his soft fur! You loved to bury your deformed nails in his fur . . . and how often you put your hands in his jaws! You played with him as with a toy, an inanimate object."

At this moment I touched Kzradock's chest. He was about to cry out, but in the same instant he sighed and let out his gathered breath. Before he began to speak again, I heard one of the candle cuffs in my big chandelier crackle.

"Do you see everything and everyone only as objects? Is that your secret?

"Look, here at the scene of the murders your puma was lying under the divan! Lady Florence . . . at that moment I believed that he still did your bidding, and I silently accused you. I hadn't thought about Ulysse Vanil and his friends . . .

"Terrible, to see it all again, recollection after recollection! How the short police second inspector gapes at the big predator, which is slowly turning toward him. He is afraid and turns pale . . . he is about to step back . . . he doesn't know where to turn or how he should conduct his investigation in this case.

"Blinded by blood! Who understands this feeling? Everything is red . . . flows red . . . all light reflects red into our eyes; everywhere we see a red mist. God, how happy I was until this moment! And how calm my nerves must have been! I had heard nothing of this murderous deed, and I lived near the studio, only one floor below. Evenings I had often heard Alice and Yvonne come home . . . Then heard no more. The two friends walked so lightly.

"And to think—it was this morning! It was the concierge who shouted for me . . . What a voice! I shudder at the thought of it. It was as sharp as the blade of a saw. The concierge had heard cries for help from the studio and had hurried upstairs. Then she had called for her husband, and then me . . . then the entire house.

"The terrible screams . . .

"The concierge had stood at the studio door and had heard Yvonne shout . . . had heard her shout these strange words: 'There are three hundred fathoms of water . . . No, it's no use . . . there are three hundred fathoms of water!'

"And then a single scream . . . and nothing more.

"The concierge stood at the door as I rushed up. Her husband came up the stairs. The good Duran had his nightcap pulled down over his ears and was wearing black cotton stockings. We stood trembling at the door. No more sounds came from inside the studio. Duran clasped his hands, then took his nightcap off his head and wound it between his fingers like a rosary.

"The murderer must still be inside!

"Oh, God! The short police inspector no doubt thought so, too, as he stood with his full detachment: a doctor and two guards . . . There he stood in the face of the two victims of such an astonishing crime. And under the divan lay the puma, apparently exhausted. But inside the small room beyond the studio the murderer must be found! . . . I looked at the thoughtful face of the police inspector. He was in terrible straits. What should he do?

"I see how he summons up his courage and makes a swift decision.

"He moves swiftly through the studio to open the door to the back room. And he seizes the handle. Good God . . . look at the puma! He is beginning to creep out from under the divan. He fixes his stare, his amber-yellow eyes on the policeman, he takes aim, his tail writhing . . . the long, smooth body is in sinuous movement; his hindquarters prepare for a jump. The police inspector has turned around . . . In an instant he understands the danger that threatens him. His arms sink down, his mouths twists into a terrible, hopeless smile . . . It all has happened so quickly that he has no thought of resistance.

"Death is certain.

"See how the dreadful animal's wildness has been awakened at the sight of the man approaching the door. See how the puma takes aim, slowly, carefully, even solemnly, but with a touch of laziness and vanity in its lithe body.

"Now! Now!

"What is happening?

"At that moment we hear a scream from downstairs, the scream of a woman calling for help. It rings shrilly through the open door from one of the lower floors. And the scream is followed by a wild plea.

"'Help! Help! I am being murdered! Help . . . me!'"

"The puma springs. But not at the inspector. Without us noticing, the beast had turned its head at the first scream, and now it springs haphazardly into the middle of the room. It lands in the pool of blood, which sprays up onto Alice's corpse. The puma, all four of its legs up to the knees in blood, pauses there a moment. It appears to listen to the shouts from below . . . An ecstatic shudder ripples through the puma. And suddenly the puma jumps again—toward us! Toward the guards, the doctor, and me.

"Heaven take pity on us!

"But the beast does not see us. He runs toward us, runs between our shaking legs . . . out onto the landing . . . and springs down the stairs in long, high leaps.

"From below the plea still sounds: 'Help . . . me! Help . . . me!'"

"Then I understand: It is Lady Florence's voice.

"And I . . . I . . . I . . ."

Here Kzradock let out another wild scream . . . foam came from his mouth and in a sudden, violent fit he threw himself off the sofa onto the floor. I took the dagger from him and removed the bandages from his hands and feet. He grew quieter, and it didn't take long before he opened his eyes and looked around. His expression was uncertain, and his pupils seemed to breathe under the influence of the candles . . . Suddenly he sighed deeply, gathered himself to a degree, and said, to my great surprise, clearly and precisely, these mystical words: "Under the water! Under the narrow riverbed of the Seine!"

III

A KNOCK — WITH STENTORIAN VOICE — THE BANISTER STANDS FIRM — THE MYSTERIOUS RING OF THE TELEPHONE — TWO WORK TOGETHER — UNDER ORDERS — MOULIN DE LA GALETTE — THE LIVING PICTURE — THE POLICEMAN'S BADGE — IN SAFETY

———————

A moment passed. And Kzradock spoke again, slowly and hesitantly, but with imperious and clear emphasis, those strange words: "Under the river! Under the narrow riverbed of the Seine!"

There was a knock at the door.

A shudder passed through both of us. It was as if this light tap on the door had brought Kzradock's tale to life. The darkness in the room thickened around us and became as tangible as a physical weight. The hair stood up on my head, and sweat came from all my pores.

And at the same moment the telephone on my desk began to ring . . .

In the darkness I heard that Kzradock was approaching the door. I involuntarily let out a shout, the door opened, and in the flickering glow of the gaslights outside I saw a form hurry away, down the steps that led to the Hall of Pain.

Kzradock had opened the door. As if magically drawn by that which hurried away, he went to the stairs, bent over the flimsy banister, and called in a stentorian voice that echoed through the halls and stairways, "Ulysse, is that you? Ulysse . . . brother in misfortune . . . I'm coming now, alive or dead!"

I saw that Kzradock was about to throw himself over the banister. I could not cover the distance quickly enough to prevent it. Good council was precious here, and only my insight into psychological phenomena instantly provided the necessary help. I pulled the table-cloth from the table so that the books, tobacco tin and vase all fell to the floor, and I kicked the shelf so that most of its contents crashed down. The racket caused Kzradock to turn his deathly pale face toward me. I caught his eye and quietly and coolly drew in the threads of his wild thoughts. My eyes locked on his, I went to him, took him by the shoulders, and shook him like a bottle whose liquid needed to be mixed. "Kzradock!" I whispered.

There he stood, shaking with cold and sorrow, his head leaning back over the banister, over the abyss, into which he had wanted to throw himself just a moment before. And he tried to free his eyes from the bonds I used to keep him with the living: my eyes. Through a tremendous effort he succeeded . . . With the force of his entire body he threw himself backward, and his head, his hair flying, described an arc through the air. But I threw myself against his legs and pinned him against the creaking banister. And there he hung. If I lessened the pressure he would fall. It was impossible for me to overpower him alone.

I shouted for help.

Lucien and Charles, my two attendants, came to assist me, and soon Kzradock sat on the stairs, entirely limp and exhausted. I knew from experience that he would now be calm, and that I could safely leave him alone . . . He was ripe for a period of isolation. I gave the attendants my orders. They should take Kzradock to his cell, and then look into who had knocked on my door earlier. The attendants assured me that neither they nor any other attendant had knocked. They had all been gathered in an empty cell in the Hall of Pain playing Zanzibar. Then who had knocked? It couldn't have been a patient . . . but who?

I had not the slightest idea and was dead tired from the experiences of the afternoon. So I left the question to my attendants, and went back to my room, where everything lay topsy-turvy. The floor was a mottled confusion of books, manuscripts, tobacco, and broken glass, and on the sofa lay the Egyptian dagger and the bandages Kzradock had been bound with. A lovely sight! My room had been transformed into a madman's cell, where evil spirits played their games.

Nevertheless, I was not discontent. While I reordered my possessions, just as one might put a mental state to right, I thought through the situation properly and made my plans. I would concern myself with investigating the crimes that formed the basis of Kzradock's state. But these investigations must be carried out with much caution: Kzradock himself was perhaps implicated, and the meddling of the police could be dangerous. I didn't want to actually hand my patient over to the police; that was in conflict with my sense of honor and my professional conscience. In my field, I have always valued the special, exception cases, because I love my science, which reduces people to their most basic elements.

But do not think that I have forgotten the essence of my art, the healing, in favor of the purely scientific aspects. I am convinced that in using my science I can learn to understand Kzradock, and so cure him and perhaps send him back into society (all of us who make up society are, after all, guilty parties), out of which he came, although he, with his bitter, aching soul, has forgotten it.

If only I were capable of doing so! I love Kzradock with all the affection of my innate nature and my years of study joined together. If I could only find this exiled soul a home and the right ground, which . . . and what did he call himself, after all, in his disjointed talk a while ago? An onion? And he was right. Behind the wilted and half-wilted onionskin his human soul lies in a lethargic state, like a seed that needs sun and care. Kzradock the Onion Man . . . should I try to find your true self and bring it back into the sunlight? Yes, then there will be no more talk of lies, only of the truth—one that will become universally known: that science has saved a soul!

My thoughts were interrupted by the telephone ringing again.

This time I picked up the receiver. The Chief of the Criminal Division of the Police Department wished to speak to me personally.

"Dear Dr. Renard de Montpensier," he said in his disciplined and always so confidential-sounding voice, "you are certainly a busy man. When I called you half an hour ago a crashing as if from an earthquake came through the telephone. I became quite concerned and uneasy, and have only now risked calling again. Unfortunately, I must bother you with something . . . It concerns a matter of great importance, a matter that I must partially put into your hands . . . Are you free this evening?"

I didn't want to have anything to do with the police just then so I answered, "It depends . . ."

The voice of the police chief took on a note of urgency. He sounded as if he were speaking directly into my ear.

"You must not say no! You must speak with me, you must place yourself at my disposal. I think it is also a matter that will interest you. I will provide you with a highly interesting patient. A genuine rarity, Doctor . . . Something unique, believe me. Yes, you know that I do not care for abnormal criminals; they always make me feel unsettled. I am not a clinician. This case, however, is absolutely something for you . . . Now are you interested?"

I must confess that I sneered at the Chief of the Criminal Division. Luckily he couldn't see through the telephone. "Couldn't you give me more information?"

The chief first mumbled something I couldn't understand. Then I heard, "Well . . . I might, reluctantly, hand over a more detailed report . . . But we can fill in all the details another day."

"This all sounds very mysterious," I said. "And your behavior seems to me very unusual."

"Unfortunately it is necessary," was his laconic reply . . . "God knows I would love it if those involved could be arrested. But that is not advisable, in fact, not even feasible."

"What do you want from me?" I asked, somewhat interested.

"I would greatly appreciate it," he replied—and his inflection clearly identified him as a police chief—"if, in an hour, you could be present outside the small movie theater that lies near the Moulin de la Galette in Montmartre. You will hardly be acquainted with this theater but you will find it easily enough. There you will meet one of my lieutenants—Monsieur Carbonel, whom you know . . . What will further take place I am not permitted to divulge. But I guarantee you will find it entertaining. It should prove both exciting and interesting. In the meantime, I will leave it to Monsieur Carbonel to be your guide. There is just one thing I would like to ask of you: you must bring a revolver! Not to defend yourself—I don't believe that will be necessary—but the revolver is absolutely essential."

This angered me. "Bring my revolver . . . ? Never!"

"You must!"

"Why do I need to bring it?"

"To shoot . . ."

"Never!"

The police chief laughed; the telephone itself actually brayed.

"But it will be fun!"

"How can that be?"

"Take the revolver with you. You'll see . . ."

I wanted to hang up, but the chief went on: "It is, as I say, a very important matter. And I am anxious that you should leave at once. You have a good hour to get there if you leave now."

At that moment I remembered Kzradock and the riddle I was hoping to solve. If I went along with this, perhaps I would be allowed—as a kind of service in return—to look at some reports that would not otherwise be made available to me. With this in mind, I said, "I will come. But I will leave my revolver at home . . ."

The chief began to shout. "No, don't do that! Pay attention to what I'm saying: cooperation between the two of you will have twice the effect . . . And with that, adieu and goodbye."

He hung up.

And then it happened as it had to happen. I obeyed, as if I had received an order . . . obeyed just as Kzradock and as any other man would have obeyed. We all obey . . . It is just as Kzradock had said in his prophetic Indian language: We obey the laws of the seed! He was right, we all are obedient, one as much as another. We are all under orders.

I grabbed my hat and coat and, reluctantly, my revolver, and was soon in the middle of the throng of Paris. I swayed through the illuminated and nearly overheated streets of Paris on the top deck of a bus. The streets smelled like a beehive full of honey. Here everything is like an eternal painting that dissolves itself daily and confidently reforms in the newest fashion, in devotion to the moment. Not even in a manic mind could a picture change as quickly as it does here. And yet the mystery of Paris lies not at all in its speed. One forgets that. Its loveliness, its eternal charm, is what remains in one's memory. And what finally remains, that is the reality.

Oh, yes, I could spend all of my time, live my entire life on the top deck of a Parisian bus. But my place is inside, in the van where the patients sit. The fact that there is something called sickness pains me twice over here in the streets, looking out as if from the seat of a carriage going forward through the splendor of the world.

We had been traveling along the boulevard quite a while and had entered Montmartre. What kind of expedition had I gotten myself involved in? And, in the meantime, my poor sick friend Kzradock sits in his cell and waits for his liberation; not from death, but from life.

Stop!

Well . . . following to my instructions, I went to the Moulin de la Galette . . . to the mill . . . high above, and blown by the mill's vanes, light meal is ground between a pair of millstones while young Parisians dance in and out of the mill below, in and out under the imperturbably white electric lamps that all obey the commands of a machine in the city . . . It had been a long time since I paid a visit to the ballroom in the mill. But I didn't go in on this night, either . . . I had a quite different goal.

A little further up the street lay the small movie theater . . . I could see its lit sign. The street here is so steep that it looks as if the signs are hung at an angle . . . There in front of the entrance stood Monsieur Carbonel. I recognized him by his smoothly shaven face and by his hawk's eyes. Those had spotted me long before; I felt that distinctly as he came toward me. "So, here you are! I knew you would come! So you thought of me, my friend . . . But you also have obeyed, you also stand here by command. Two orders have brought about our meeting."

He extended his hand to me, and I extended mine. And I allowed myself to give him a questioning look.

"A new bill tonight," he said casually, as if we were regulars. "Is there something you would like to see, Doctor?"

I looked at the placard and thought, God, this is a matter of such complete indifference to me! I said to Monsieur Carbonel, who had fallen into conversation with someone, "What should we do, really?"

"We should go in," said the clever Monsieur Carbonel. "It is time. Because I believe that tonight will also not be successful . . . we want to sit as far to the rear as possible."

The lieutenant suddenly looked me straight in the eyes: "You did bring your revolver with you?"

"Yes," I grumbled, like a schoolboy. Monsieur Carbonel merely nodded.

We went in.

The room inside is completely dark and filled with the smell of garlic. It is obviously a poor crowd, which is in the habit of coming here. The darkness prevents me from seeing them.

A desert picture is showing. A caravan of camels travels across the sand. Sand is everywhere, only sand. The big animals sway side to side like sluggish ships. Although their eyes watch everything, they have a terrible, dull expression. It is the melancholy of the animal kingdom, I say to myself; the working class possesses a similar melancholy. But how could they feel otherwise . . .

The picture vanishes and it is light in the room. I see that the audience was mixed, as I had thought. Two rows in front of us, in fact, sit some more elegant patrons.

"Hang it all!" whispered Monsieur Carbonel, after he had bought a program and had had a look at it. "We have come none too early! Do you have your revolver ready? When I say 'now,' take it out of your jacket pocket. And when I say 'fire,' shoot it. Is your revolver loaded?"

"No," I whispered to him, and smiled maliciously at my small triumph.

"It doesn't matter," replied the lieutenant. "I took the precaution of bringing two . . . I will give you one . . ."

I looked at Monsieur Carbonel and stammered, "But whom? What? What should I shoot at?"

"Shoot at the puma!"

"At the puma . . . ?"

"Yes!" Then Monsieur Carbonel told me to be quiet. He stood up, but sat back down again.

It was dark, and the new picture began.

But what was that? It seemed to me that I knew this scene . . . the small studio, the two young women lying on the floor, the police inspector who just this moment enters . . .

"What's the name of this picture?" I muttered breathlessly.

"*The Mysterious Murder*," replied Monsieur Carbonel, and at the same time he pressed a revolver into my hands . . .

Yes, now I see it . . . and I experience it again in memory . . . there under the sofa lies the puma . . . now the inspector approaches the door. The beast is at the point of creeping out . . . now it prepares to spring . . .

and it leaps into the middle of the room, so that the pool of blood splashes high . . .

"Fire!" whispers Monsieur Carbonel.

And he fires his own revolver. Instinctively I obey and fire as well.

A dreadful commotion arises in the theater . . . the living picture remains motionless; the predator, now torn into pieces by the bullets, is frozen in its leap toward the door.

At that moment the lights come on. In the midst of the wild, screaming crowd Monsieur Carbonel jumps onto a chair and holds up his badge.

"Close the doors!" he cries.

Monsieur Carbonel looks around with his hawk's eyes . . . and it is so quiet that I can hear my heart beat.

Among the elegant clique a young man has dropped to the floor, helpless . . . in his fall he has frantically clung to his hat. Monsieur Carbonel climbs down from the chair and goes over to him. He snatches the hat from him with a quick jerk . . .

"Well, Fräulein," he says with a satisfied smile, "I have succeeded in finding you! Did you believe that it was Ulysse Vanil and his cronies who fired the shots? No, it was only me . . . and Dr. Renard de Montpensier, my companion, who will now take you to a place where you can feel safe."

IV

THE BLACK RATS — THE GUARDIAN OF JUSTICE — IN
THE AUTOMOBILE — MISTER WELLS — THE AMERICAN'S
RESIGNATION — TWO RATS — SWEAR! — THE SAVING OF
THE SOUL — FLOWERS AND FRUIT — IT'S ON FIRE!

———————

In no time things were sorted out. Monsieur Carbonel held firm, even as the audience attacked us. I remember that I had the impression that the people looked like black rats as they rushed toward us. The police are hated, I thought with satisfaction, as they should be . . . In the devil's name, knock him down, the damned sneak! At the same time I prepared not only to defend myself, but also Monsieur Carbonel and our prisoner, if it should come to that. Man is a complicated creature.

As I said, Monsieur Carbonel held firm and stared them down with his eyes, like two glowing lanterns, acting as the guardian of justice. He backed out of the room and drew the entire swarm of people along behind him. On the street he stopped, and the others immediately did the same. He directed—so help me God—the entire crowd, all those who hated him, merely by suggestion, because he had a strong will and knew what he was doing. If he had given them an order to shout, they would have obeyed him. But he was satisfied with whistling for a cab. It came quickly, and pulled up in a sharp curve to the front of the theater. We put our prisoner inside without difficulty. As soon as the crowd was free of Carbonel's gaze, it surrounded the cab. Faces pressed against the windows on all sides; sticks and umbrellas were raised up against us threateningly. "Windows up!" shouted Monsieur Carbonel. "The people are quite insane tonight. The murder scene has gone to their heads, and they have turned into wildcats."

The driver blew his horn and the car began slowly to move.

I looked closely at our prisoner. To my great amazement he sat there smiling. I saw that the lieutenant was also surprised at this. The cab drove quickly downhill toward the boulevard that led away. The lantern light on the sloping street that flashed over our faces created quick, sudden pictures of moments that were just as suddenly followed by darkness. But whenever the face of the stranger was lit up, I saw the same cunning look. An unconcerned, haughty, victorious smile . . .

For a long while it was quiet in the cab. To all appearances we were relaxed. But this calm was a sham. The others were undoubtedly at least as anxious and alert as I was. All three of us had things to say to one another, and perhaps just for that reason we were quiet. In the end, Monsieur Carbonel broke the silence, and at the same time he took his cigarette case out of his pocket. I saw that he also smiled, as if he wanted to outbid the other with a more triumphant smile, one which nearly bared his teeth.

"It was a mistake for you to be here tonight," he said to our prisoner. "Don't look for an excuse. We'll call it a mistake. Agreed?"

The stranger broke into laughter that sounded not at all forced, and he answered in English: "As you wish! You can feel free to call it a mistake . . . That is no doubt the case. And I am at least as curious as you about what will emerge from this mistake. Were it a little brighter in this cab you would perhaps sport a less arrogant smile, Monsieur Carbonel . . . You believe you have captured the central figure of a tragedy . . . Do you know who I am?"

Monsieur Carbonel leaned forward. Even in the uncertain light I saw that he had gone pale, almost bloodless. He bent over the stranger's face, who, still smiling, now continued: "Do you see who I am? Did you really believe that you were to be granted the privilege of arresting Lady Florence? No, I have not granted you that. If you thought that I would, you really don't know Mister Wells!"

The stranger raised his right hand to his head. When his hand came back down it held a wig, and he now showed very closely cropped fiery red hair, perhaps the reddest hair I had ever seen. Mister Wells's hair color was not to be mistaken; his hair looked almost like blood that had sprayed over his skull after a violent blow to the head. Monsieur Carbonel laughed bitterly, almost sobbing . . . gulping the air with wild swallows and odd animal sounds. Then he shouted, "But she was there as well!"

"Certainly," answered Mister Wells. "She was there as well. But I, I wanted to . . . You poached on my preserve, Monsieur Carbonel. I console myself with the fact that tonight I have displayed the finest quality an American can have: not courage, not cleverness, but resignation! Resignation is the final quality that we Americans have to cultivate. All other qualities are innate in us, but resignation must be acquired . . . And I am proud of the fact that in the matter of Lady Florence I have continually demonstrated resignation. I have nearly reached my goal. I would consider it an honor, Monsieur Carbonel, if you would help me with the fulfillment of my plan . . . I would very much welcome your assistance. But as a typical American, I must interpret every question as a racial problem, and approach it as such. If you will help me capture Lady Florence, she will be in our hands by early morning . . . Would you be willing to act in my service, Monsieur Carbonel, just for tonight? And to that end also join in my resignation . . . a genuine Gallic resignation, to which I have appealed to on earlier occasions, and never in vain . . . The iron must be struck while it is hot; we must take advantage of the moment! We must try to bring this matter, which becomes more enigmatic by the day, to a reasonable conclusion . . . I am not a religious man . . . in no way am I devout . . . but this is a matter that concerns the well-being of my soul. In spite of everything, I have kept a sure trust in human nature. In any case, her riddle can be solved! And I must solve this riddle, because Lady Florence exists. I have seen her three times, the last being tonight. The first two times she vanished in quite inexplicable ways. I will tell you about it some time, Monsieur Carbonel."

Mister Wells was suddenly quiet. And just as suddenly he seized the French detective's right hand and raised it high. At that moment we were traveling along the wide boulevard along which the human current passed as if to a secret march melody, a melancholy, ambling music . . .

"Swear!" cried Mister Wells. "And you swear as well, Dr. Renard de Montpensier . . . swear to reveal nothing of what I will now tell you! Our lives may be at stake, and even more so, our eternal spiritual balance . . . And promise me above all that tonight we will stay together, because tonight something will happen."

Monsieur Carbonel and I nodded our heads toward Mister Wells's red hair, which from time to time flamed in the lantern light. But Mister Wells was too occupied with his thoughts to notice our attentiveness and excitement.

"Yes," he said. "Tell me you agree! No . . . swear, swear!"

And he suddenly regarded us with wide pupils. We nodded in agreement, and Monsieur Carbonel, who seemed to have forgotten his earlier disappointment, pressed Mister Wells's hand and said, "Tonight belongs to America . . . But if your plans fail, tomorrow we will have our turn."

"Good," agreed Mister Wells. "That's as it should be." Then he turned to me and said, in a tone that suggested he thought I could not be very bright, "Do you fear being robbed of your night's rest, Dr. Renard de Montpensier? Because the night will pass in an extremely odd way. I have a notion that this matter will also interest you. Do you know Kzradock?"

"He is my patient," I answered. "In the interest of making a more correct diagnosis of his condition I have most willingly sacrificed many nights of sleep."

"Just as I thought," murmured Mister Wells. "You have also been drawn into this matter . . . We all stand at the gate to this hell of the passions, to this underworld of horrors which make me shudder . . . And, nevertheless, I feel I must enter! As do you! As does Monsieur Carbonel! We are, so to speak, conspirators, and all hope that the light of reason will see us through the galleries of darkness which we face . . . Tell me, Dr. Renard de Montpensier, what have you discovered through your examinations of Kzradock?"

I felt my face turning red. As luck would have it, we were then on a dark street, and I made use of that darkness. I wanted to betray nothing, because I myself was, in a way, a member of a secret police. So I lied: "I have not yet gotten beyond my initial examinations. Kzradock interests me, and furthermore he is a very sympathetic patient. I don't deny that he very much occupies my thoughts. More precisely, I dare not answer. I have my suspicions . . . and that's all! But tell me, Mister Wells, where do you intend us to spend the night? Where would you have us go?"

"You need not give the driver a new address," replied Mister Wells. "Something will happen tonight at your institution. The drama will play out there. You have a reception room where we can wait, do you not? Do you object to us using it as our headquarters? I think Lady Florence will arrive in about three hours. Is your reception room very far from Kzradock's room? Not far? Good. Do you believe that he will be asleep when we get there?"

"I think so," I replied. "He was so troubled the entire afternoon that he should now be sleeping the sleep of the just."

"If he isn't sleeping you will have to give him a sleeping powder," said Mister Wells. "But a mild one, because he should be able to wake up if we call him."

I tried to express my doubts in regard to Mister Wells's argument.

"You believe that Lady Florence will force her way into my institute in the middle of the night? That is impossible. She would not be able to enter."

"She'll come," replied Mister Wells. "But we might not get to see her. Everything will depend upon whether we design our plans with enough skill . . . How many stories does your building have? Three?"

"With the raised ground floor, four . . ."

"Of course. And Kzradock's cell is on the second floor?"

"No, the first."

"Then I have miscalculated. Where is your reception room?"

"On the second floor."

"That is unfortunate," responded Mister Wells. "We must arrange ourselves accordingly. Listen: You must have two or three attendants stay up tonight. And I will instruct these attendants precisely how they are to behave. In addition, you will have to make sure we will have three or four large bed sheets at our disposal. And, finally, you must have a cell prepared. This cell should be decorated in a regal manner, with the best furniture and bedding the institute possesses. It should be decorated with flowers, and the table should be set for five people, with fruit and wine set out. Can all this be seen to?"

"I don't think that flowers and fruit are to be found at the institute."

"Then both must be obtained. They are necessary. You certainly have a telephone in your institute. We can call one of the all-night restaurants on the boulevard and order the missing items.

"Why should the table be set for five people?" I asked, and Mister Wells gaped at me.

"Either it will be five or it will be none," was his answer.

At that moment the cab came to a stop—at the entrance to the street on which I have lived for so many years.

"Why aren't we moving?" I called to the window behind the driver.

"The street is closed off," the young driver replied laconically.

"What's wrong?"

The driver leaned toward me. "I believe there is a roof fire . . . It is burning just across from the lunatic asylum. The street is full of hoses and firemen."

"A roof fire!" roared Mister Wells. "Then she is certainly already there. I know her tracks when they appear . . . know her talent for deflecting attention . . . On! On! Your driver can get his money tomorrow . . . And pay attention! All of our lives may be at stake! We must stay together! Don't leave us, Dr. Renard de Montpensier . . . and let's hope we can reach the institute!

All three of us stormed out of the cab, as if we were twenty-year-olds and all this was about nothing more than a foolish prank.

"What is burning?" shouted Mister Wells to the chain of firemen who were blocking the street, and who, to a man, all lifted their hands to their caps when they saw Monsieur Carbonel.

"The insane asylum is burning," they all answered together, as if on command.

V

THE TENSE ORDEAL — YOU ARE LYING! — THE BADGE — ON THE WAY! — THE PATIENT HAS ESCAPED — REVOLUTION — CHAOS — THE PALE FACES — THE HANDS — NARCOTIC VAPORS — MISSING

───────

"Repeat that!" I roared like a wild animal at the firemen. "Repeat that! What did you say?"

"The madhouse is burning," one replied laconically.

I rushed as if possessed, as if I were myself an escaping patient. And in my wake the two secret policemen raced forward like tracking dogs. I ran over coils of fire hoses that resembled the intestines of a butchered mythical beast.

Close to the entrance of the asylum stood the steam-sprayer, with the heated kettle underneath, and with the violent kick of the pump and shaking, a dense steam spewed forth from the stack.

The asylum itself was dark . . . as if deserted.

There was no fire to be seen.

As we were about to force our way through the gate, the fire chief stepped into our path, grabbed me by the arm and said, "Where are you going?"

"I am the chief doctor of the Institute," I replied. "Don't you know me ... Dr. Renard de Montpensier? For God's sake, let me go in!"

"Go no further!" ordered the chief, and he used his body to block the narrow passage between the hose coils that led to the gate.

"Make way for Dr. Renard de Montpensier!" I shouted. "My honor and my life are at stake! My records are in danger! The lives of my patients are in danger! Everything that is dear to me is in danger. Make way, you idiotic lackey! Make way, you uniformed fool! God forgive my anger, but I am livid ..."

I was nearly sobbing with rage. The fire chief looked at me mockingly.

"You are lying," he said.

"I'm what?" I asked, baffled. "I'm lying?"

"Yes, indeed," replied the fire chief, and he waved a couple of firefighters over to help. "You are lying; you are not Dr. Renard de Montpensier. It is good that we found you. Because you are obviously an escaped patient. As far as Dr. Renard de Montpensier is concerned, I spoke with him only a moment ago. He is directing rescue efforts."

I turned to Monsieur Carbonel and said, "Would you tell this man who I am ..."

Monsieur Carbonel took out his badge and identified himself.

The chief took the badge and examined it thoroughly. Then he said, "Well ... this identification is certainly real. But it is stolen. I spoke about this very thing with Monsieur Carbonel. And he told me that his identification was stolen in the turmoil as the patients were escaping."

I felt faint. It was as if the ground had slipped away from beneath my feet. I stammered, "But then what is happening in my institute?"

With a threatening air, Monsieur Carbonel took a step toward the fire chief. "If you will fetch one of your men," he said, "you will see who I am."

The fire chief barely shook his head. "I'm not about to hold things up for some fool," he said. "And tell me this: Who does your third person believe himself to be?" And he pointed at Mister Wells.

A vengeful smile came over Monsieur Carbonel's face, and he said, "Chief, this man can serve as a fit offering to your powers of discernment. He is in reality one of the escaped patients whom we have captured. A mad Englishman who suffers from a persecution complex. He believes he is a member of the American secret police, and needs to be put under lock and key. Keep him in custody and don't let him escape. He is dangerous. We, however, demand free passage, in the name of the law and of justice."

At that moment Mister Wells really did look like a madman. His hat was in his hand, and his red hair glowed in the uncertain light. He threw himself at Monsieur Carbonel. Two firemen rushed over and my two companions were separated.

Monsieur Carbonel took a small whistle out of his pocket and put it to his lips. Two piercing whistles shrilled through the night. He put the whistle back into his pocket, crossed his arms over his chest, and stood waiting and listening.

From the courtyard and from both sides of the street we heard the sound of running feet, and in a few moments three firemen ran out of the darkness. As they caught sight of Monsieur Carbonel, all three raised their hands to their caps.

"Do you know me?" asked Monsieur Carbonel.

All three men nodded.

"Then would you be so kind as to introduce me to this gentleman," said Mister Carbonel. "He deserves to know my name."

The firemen said his name.

The fire chief went white. He stammered. "I don't understand any of this . . ."

"Do you wish more proof?" asked Monsieur Carbonel. "Apparently one cannot ask comprehension of a fire chief! But console yourself with the fact that it's not every day that you come across an insane asylum in flames . . . And now, tell me where the fire is!"

"Fire?" replied the fire chief. "There is no fire here! If you're in the secret police I don't understand why you don't have better information."

"There's no fire here!" I cried. "Monsieur Carbonel, did you hear what he said? He has given me back my life. No fire here. My institute is not burning . . . My expensive books are not being consumed by flames . . . Everything can still be set right! Is this really true, Chief? There is no fire?"

"No fire," replied the fire chief. "But there is a revolution."

"A revolution?"

"That's right. Sad but true. The patients have installed an emperor. That's why the hoses had to be brought in."

"Let us in," I cried. "They will understand me. They will obey me!"

"They are in control of the building on the far side of the garden," the fire chief continued. "We have set up ladders there, and the battle will be directed from there . . . Firemen and policemen are fighting with patients inside the building . . . At the beginning, the patients lit red Bengal lights that lit up the entire building. Heaven knows where they got the fireworks. But now everything has sunk into darkness, and the fighting goes on in the dark. Some of the patients fled into the garden, where the man who called himself Dr. Renard de Montpensier is talking to them. I thought he was trying to calm them down. Now I know better. He must be the one who is stirring up the patients."

"That's horrible," I cried. "How will this end?"

"Let's go in. The sooner the better. We'll take these three firemen with us," said Monsieur Carbonel.

"I'm going, too!" roared Mister Wells.

Monsieur Carbonel smiled and, turning to the chief, said, "You are responsible to me for this man. He is my patient, an incurable victim of the Detective Hallucination of the Anglo-Saxon race. Treat him with respect, and spray him with a little water if he gets prickly."

Monsieur Carbonel continued to smile, the fire chief laughed, and Mister Wells gritted his teeth. Tears rolled down his cheeks.

"Let me in," I screamed. "I can't bear this any longer!"

Mister Wells tried all possible ways to escape from the fire chief. He punched and butted his red skull against the stomachs of the firemen who surrounded him. But in vain! He had been outwitted . . . Monsieur Carbonel laughed heartily over his victory while we hurried through the courtyard and ran up the main staircase of the building. I ran without looking up. My heart pounded, and I was barely in control of myself.

As we came into the entrance hall, I immediately understood the extent of the disaster. The struggle had obviously raged here first. A barricade had been made from chairs, mattresses, bedding, and old junk. Everything lay in a jumble, and on the stairs lay broken chair legs, shards of glass, and torn curtains.

I paused, startled and amazed. Who had the power to stage all of this, and how could it happen behind my back? What end had all this served? And how could I find the right threads in all of mysteries that had swept over me in a single day?

I thought of Kzradock—I think I spoke his name aloud. He provided me, to some extent, with a weak conjecture, a hope of understanding, the premonition of a solution.

Could it be him?

Suddenly I heard a sound, and I flinched. What was that? An odd trickle . . . Ah, now I understood. It was water from the hoses that had been used on the patients. I rushed up the steps and Monsieur Carbonel followed me. We ran down a long corridor without encountering anyone. The doors to the cells stood wide open, and the wind that rushed in through the broken window panes billowed out the curtains. Then I heard whimpering coming from one of the cells.

I stopped and went inside.

On the bed lay a bound and gagged attendant.

When he saw me, his eyes almost popped out of their sockets. I went to him, released his gag, loosened his bonds and asked in my most commanding voice, with which I took immediate charge in the cell, "How did this happen?"

The attendant pulled out a cotton wad that had been stuck deep in his mouth. After he spat a few times, he began to give his account.

The uprising began just after my departure from the institute. The attendants were surrounded by ten of the strongest patients, bound and gagged, and thrown into empty cells. Only one managed to escape, and it was he

who had called the police and the fire department . . .
The patients had gone about the execution of their plan
very rationally, and only the energy they had displayed
during the mutiny pointed to the abnormal mental abili-
ties which had been set in motion . . . I received an answer of great value: none of my patients had been the
leader of the turmoil.

A stranger had had his hand in it.

I asked the attendant to follow me, and we went further into the male wing—Monsieur Carbonel, the three
firemen, the attendant, and I.

It was strangely quiet in this wing, despite its being
in the midst of the turmoil. But this was due to all the
soundproof doors. We were approaching the wing by the
garden. Only a long, narrow hall still separated us from
it. What would happen if my patients caught sight of
me? How would they react? And what should I do to
calm them?

The fire chief came running along the hall.

"Where are the patients?" I shouted to him.

"There are no more patients in the building," he answered, and he stopped. "They are gathered in the garden and are now completely surrounded."

"How many women are there?" I asked.

"They are all there," answered the fire chief. "And
they are the most zealous ones of all. They have given us
the most hell."

"Let's hurry down there," I said to Mister Carbonel.

"It's hard to get there that way," said the fire chief. "Follow me."

"Nothing is as important as my patients," I said. "I must at least see them."

And I ran down the hall and quickly reached the wing next to the garden. Through the window at the end of the hall that looked out over the lawn I saw the most pathetic gathering I have ever seen. There stood my patients, in their institutional clothes, surrounded by firemen and police. Some screamed like wild animals, others sang, a shrill and melancholy sound.

They formed a restless human sea. Their guards had lit three smoky torches, which threw a ghostly light on the tormented faces. From time to time one of them tried to break out of the circle, only to be forcibly thrown back. Pity filled my heart at the sight! I knew well the fate of these people, and I understood them. It was as if I looked out on all the worries and suffering of the world, which had been herded together by a tight police cordon . . .

But where was the will that had driven these people to rise up?

Monsieur Carbonel and the others—excepting the fire chief—had followed me. They all stood at the window, silent, as if under a spell. They were all shaken by this horrific sight. I had to go down there, or my heart would break in despair. A fire ladder was leaning against the window ledge where I stood. In spite of the protests of the others, I wanted to make use of the ladder, in order to hurry to the garden. I was already standing in the window frame when the fire chief came running back.

"Come help me," he shouted.

"What is it?" we all cried, on edge as we were, and we followed him back the way he had come.

He rushed through the building, upstairs and downstairs, through the Rotunda of Hope, along the Hall of Pain . . .

He stopped at Kzradock's room.

"Smoke is coming from this room," the fire chief said.

He gripped the door handle. But though the door was not locked it was bolted from the inside. We tried to pry it open, without success. Between the door and the threshold I saw a thin line of smoke escaping.

"We have to get in," the fire chief shouted.

Just then a voice, melancholy as if coming from some distant place, rang out. It was a voice I knew well: Kzradock's voice. And before he spoke, I already knew what he would say: "Under the river, under the narrow riverbed of the Seine."

The fire chief pounded on the door with a short ax, but it wouldn't give way. We all tried to help by pounding on the door panels with our hands.

From inside the cell a scream rang out. And at that moment, just as the door sprang open, I noticed two hands let go of the window ledge, and we heard the fall of a body sliding down the wall.

Kzradock lay dazed in his bed. The room was filled with smoke from a brazier that stood on the floor. The smoke had a strong, hot, narcotic allure.

I ran to the window and leaned out. The stranger had apparently not injured himself in his fall.

He had disappeared.

VI

THE OCEAN OF THE SOUL — NAILED DOWN — THE HAND
ON THE TRIGGER OF THE GUN — HAVE FAITH! — THE WILD
BIRDS — THE BARREN PAMPAS — THE YOUNG PUMA —
LADY FLORENCE — THE DANCE OF DEATH

———————

I rushed to Kzradock and leaned over him.

He lay with wide-open eyes. In the weak light coming through the window his pupils were dilating and contracting convulsively, without rhythm or reason.

As I looked into his moving pupils I immediately had a strange impression, the impression of an ocean in which something was sinking, gliding to the bottom . . . a face that I thought I should know . . . Did Kzradock's eyes still hold the image of the one who had fled? Or what was this? An early memory raced through my mind while I stared at this ocean of the soul. My glance passed through his pupils as if through a telescope.

In those eyes, whose focus changed erratically, there was a drawing, attractive power that pulled my eyes, as it were, into them. But there was even more! I had the vague but certain feeling that Kzradock's soul was at this moment in direct touch with the world around us, that he had an effect on it and in turn allowed it to act on him. I felt a current of corrosive power, cold and ozone-like, pass over me. And I suddenly noticed I was paralyzed. I could not move, not my hands, not even change the direction in which I was looking. I stood as if nailed in place, stooped over Kzradock, in an awkward position, with one hand on my knee and other supported on the edge of the sofa.

A frightful terror went through me. It was as if my thoughts, horrified, flew upward and whirled about, unable to find any firm hold in the space around me. But at the same time I clearly knew that I stood in this room with Monsieur Carbonel and the fire chief. I wondered why they didn't rush over to me. Stillness reigned in the cell, and in my powerlessness I understood that the others must also be paralyzed . . . the fire chief was still standing, his hand raised, on the other side of the window; Monsieur Carbonel stood at the door, his finger on the trigger of his revolver.

As my initial fright subsided, a deep peace filled my mind. Only my body was paralyzed; my mind continued to function normally. I tried to think logically, as is my habit, but such thought was confounded by the wholly strange and unusual things I saw.

Apparently a bond had been formed between Kzradock and me that was so intimate that, with some inner vision, I saw what he felt. I knew his thoughts, I saw his visions, and what was even more astonishing, I could talk to him without moving my lips, soul to soul.

And he could answer my silent questions.

He answered my questions in a way that, truly, seemed not at all pathological or delirious as earlier, but was clear and frank.

It was his innermost self answering my innermost self. We had been seeking one another for a long time. Now we called to one another, like the deathwatch beetles who communicate—each from his hole—with a quiet knocking. That was how it felt to me. Time and space vanished; we were alone, Kzradock and I.

"Make nothing of what you may see," whispered Kzradock's soul to mine. "Believe me! Believe me! Have faith in me! Everything is visions. But have faith in me!"

"What do you want?" asked my soul.

"I want to look at my sick mind from the outside," replied Kzradock's deep inner voice. "Tell me, brother, what do you see?"

"I see the ocean," I replied. "I see the ocean. With a face in its depths. Who is that?"

"His name is Ulysse, the poor man," replied Kzradock. "He lives in me like a shadow. One moment he rises to the surface out of the waves, the next moment he sinks into the depths. Ulysse Vanil, the vanilla-seeking Ulysses, the wanderer searching for the fragrant spice in the ocean of my soul . . . But what else do you see?"

"Over the troubled ocean I can see wild birds flying, and as the storm howls they head for land. On the coast, a woman strolls in a long black gown, and the birds circle over her head in smaller and smaller arcs. Now they are flying in pairs. They bill and coo and gather the rough sandy hair-grass for their nests. But why is the woman in black weeping? Look, the waves have calmed, and everything breathes quiet."

"Such was my love," replied Kzradock. "The birds find brooding places along the coast and hatch their eggs, paying the storms no attention. My love, however, was a woman in black who wandered on the outer strands . . . Tell me, brother, what else do you see?"

"Now I see barren pampas."

"But, brother, does the woman in black remain?"

"No, the image has changed . . . I see the barren pampas . . . A puma is running with its young, and a hunter lies in wait. One of the young is caught in the trap . . . is taken to a large city . . . There it is put on a ship and travels over the ocean . . . And again the birds come flying. Now they have their young with them . . .

"The young puma, the predator, runs about tame on the deck of the ship. The woman in black is sitting there . . . One of the sailors approaches her and makes an indecent offer. She orders him to jump into the sea . . . and he does . . . and now I see how she takes the puma in her arms and kisses it and buries her nails in the animal's fur. Her eyes are full of tears, but her mouth is set in an arrogant smile that seems to have been nurtured by years-long sorrows."

"Lady Florence," whispered Kzradock. And soon after he repeated, "Lady Florence."

At this name I started. It was as if I had been running and had stumbled over a stone and now had to stop to catch my breath. A glimmer of self-realization passed through me. I vaguely understood that I was helping Kzradock explore visions that another had forbidden him to see.

Kzradock himself was in Lady Florence's power. She had sealed his mouth with seven seals so that he could not betray the secrets he knew, and now he wanted to make use of me to break her hold over him. What he did not dare to see for himself, he gave to me so I could recount it to him, and in this way bring some clarity to the dark world of images in which he lived. Bound even as a medium, he used me to release some of his strength in an attempt at breaking out of his prison.

Then I felt an unfortunate urge not to let myself be used any further. If only I had not felt this, perhaps everything would now be different. But I decided to set my will against Kzradock's own. Physically paralyzed by the power of his eyes, I took a mental attack position. Precisely at the moment when I could have solved his riddle, I became afraid! Terror made me retreat. If he succeeded in loading the entire burden of his soul onto my shoulders I was afraid that I would then have to bear Lady Florence's curse in the future!

Sparks of thought jumped through my fragile consciousness like an electric connection that breaks for a moment.

And again Kzradock asked, "What do you see, brother?"

I had a sudden inspiration. I answered clearly and firmly: "I see myself reflected in your eyes."

"You see yourself?" Kzradock asked, whimpering. "Is that true? You see yourself? Look deeply, search . . . You see nothing but yourself?"

"No," I whispered, with effort. "I see only myself in your pupils. Nothing more."

"Then you cannot save me."

My entire body trembled.

Deep inside Kzradock's eyes I saw a woman bending over a sleeping man. She kissed him, smoothed his hair, and rocked him in her arms. Then the woman took a bottle from her breast and shook the contents into his ear. She looked at him and kissed him again. She smoothed his hair, an intimate and sensitive gesture, as she watched the expression on his face. He suddenly appeared to go into convulsions. She turned away, and I was able to see her face full on. She was beautiful and pale, and her oval face was framed with splendid hair, black as the night. But she was no longer young. She looked as if she had tried to erase the signs of age from her face using cosmetics. She suddenly seized a candle. She leaned toward the bed . . . and look, look . . . she touches the flame to the quilt and the cloth catches fire . . . the entire bed is in flames . . .

"What do you see?" wailed Kzradock.

Seized again by horror I answered, "Kzradock, I see nothing."

"You are right." The words rang out from deep inside Kzradock. "Here the emptiness begins . . . here my soul dies. I feel as if the scars on my brow are burning . . . What happened . . . you didn't see? How did it happen? Was it inevitable? Did it have to happen? Where is she now? And why did she leave me? Try to penetrate down to where my thought has hidden itself. How terrible it is to be dependant on a thought which one cannot find! Be a hunter, Renard de Montpensier, take precautions: take your collecting box in hand, take your hunting knife, take everything you need . . . and go hunting in my soul, hunt the thought that has fled. Pursue it through the thickets and thorn bushes that hide it . . . And if you have to, kill it! But I would prefer that you catch it and let me see it . . . I want to satisfy myself as to how it looks . . . Bore your eyes into me . . . Search, seek, and hunt!"

Dazed and overwhelmed, I stared into Kzradock's eyes. First I saw red flames . . . they burned and flashed red and yellow. But then I suddenly beheld something that was so gruesome that I almost instantly forgot it again. It was as if the eyes of my soul had closed at the sight, as if my mind refused to accept it! I still wonder about what I actually saw. But my wondering comes to nothing.

It may be that my instantaneous forgetting was the reason that at that moment Kzradock suffered a cataleptic-hysterical attack. His body was seized by a convulsion and lifted like a bridge so that only his nape and the balls of his feet still touched the sofa. At the same time he shouted, with the full power of his lungs, "If I possess nothing else, I possess power! And I will now summon all the mad, command them all to dance!"

He leapt off the sofa and stood in the middle of the room. Another jump took him to the doorway. And as fast as a cat he ran down the Hall of Pain . . .

We followed him as if we had awakened from a mad dream. The fire chief rubbed his eyes as he ran, and Monsieur Carbonel cleared his throat as if he were hoarse. We ran on shaky legs and we could not catch Kzradock.

But he stopped at the window where we had stood earlier. A clear, deep, flute-like sound came from his breast. The sound was a bit like a cello, powerful and deep. He made the sound three times, each time with decreasing volume. The sound was summoning, luring, plaintive, imploring . . . like the cry of a bird.

We caught up to him, and I grasped his shoulder.

"Kzradock," I whispered.

But he tore loose from my grip and moved closer to the open window.

All the pale, miserable faces down below in the garden had turned toward us, as if they awaited an order.

The torches cast their light on the mad. They seemed frozen. The firemen and policemen, who waited impatiently for the command to take the mad back to their cells, had no more trouble keeping them together.

Suddenly Kzradock moved his hand, as if he were beating time. First slowly, then faster and faster he conducted. No sound came from his lips. And it was deathly quiet in the garden as well.

There followed a silent, mad minuet that I will never forget. As if they heard faraway notes, the sounds of a celebration of life, the mad began to circle one another. Without a sound, the entire crowd moved gradually into motion. Accompanied by Kzradock, who beat time from his window, the mad danced on the great grass court in the eerie torchlight. And just as we in the hallway above stood paralyzed at this new horror, so the firemen and policemen stood as if hypnotized by the dancing patients.

The dancing grew wilder and wilder, the beat faster and faster. It was like a dance macabre, a dance of spirits ... and it was also a dance of ghosts: the minuet of souls awakened back into life and made to dance there below in the darkness.

VII

THE INDESCRIBABLE — THE ABYSS OF MADNESS — THE
POWER OF THE WILL — THE EMPTINESS OF SPACE — THE
OPEN WINDOW — BROTHER! — THE SECRET MISSION —
PRINCIPLE AGAINST PRINCIPLE — AT THE THROAT

———————

I can hardly describe what occurred in the following minutes! I venture to do so only because of my confidence in the discernment of my readers. But at this moment, I cannot guarantee that what I relate is the complete truth. It is as good as impossible to reconstruct exactly what took place in that short span of time, the many impulses and sudden motives that rose to the surface. At the edge of the abyss between madness and reason language comes to a stop, and words can no longer explain . . .

What I had experienced on that singular day had, not without good reason, thrown my innermost self into wild turmoil. I had lived through crises as very few had before me: Kzradock's tale, the scene in the movie theater, and the events in my own insane asylum had all inflamed my blood and mercilessly wrung my nerves. A senseless round of changing images—and what images!—had bewildered me and made my soul shudder. All the emotions and pain, all the fear that one might ever feel, were allocated to me over the course of only a few hours. And all of them stemmed from Kzradock...

That must be understood, in order to grasp what happened next...

Standing in the darkness, I was still watching Kzradock's silhouette in the open window. Far below in the garden, with the torches illuminating the grass court, the dancing had slowed. This was because Kzradock, who beat time from the window, appeared to be dwelling on a memory that was being evoked by the melody that he had silently struck up...

I stood two paces behind him and could not move. It was as if I were paralyzed. But my mind struggled to break free, to clarify the situation for itself, to understand it, and to become its master.

And there came a moment when I felt my will begin to stir. It summoned all its power to push away my mental numbness... and at the same time it also strained to move the furthest joint of my little finger. Because my will was able to do that small thing I was no longer paralyzed. And while my brain searched through a thousand rational arguments by which it could be persuaded, my will worked on the muscles to force them to obey...

And, in the end, it succeeded.

It succeeded by way of a sudden offensive, one which made sweat appear on my brow. It fought to bend my little finger. And immediately thereafter it freed my hand. A wave of warmth passed through me: I also had an arm free! I realized that the paralysis was retreating little by little from my body. I couldn't yet move my feet, but I knew it wouldn't be long! Now I shifted my head, now raised my arm. And now, now! Now I could move, I could move my feet forward, I could go where I wished.

I now stood outside Kzradock's sphere of control.

I stood for a moment, enjoying my victory. Having my self back was a liberation. I remember that I silently called my own name. Yes, I was Dr. Renard de Montpensier, chief doctor of this insane asylum—thanks to the power of my healthy intellect in this house of insanity.

Now I understood just what the struggle with Kzradock meant! It was the struggle between madness and reason. A struggle between his insanity, which wanted to crowd into my circles, and my reason, which felt a curious desire to enter his world. How would it end, this fearful duel fought by the strongest members of mankind? The weapons looked dreadful and unevenly matched: The slender blade of reason is no more than a probe against the tomahawk of insanity, which can crush a skull with a single blow. Still, there was perhaps time enough to win the battle! One must first gain control of himself, then secure all the positions that can be secured, and only then carefully calculate one's combat strategy.

I carefully moved a step closer to Kzradock. I now stood almost directly behind his back, which was as tense as the arc of a bow. He seemed not to notice me. Then I called his name. A shudder passed through him, and his raised hand moved as if to grasp something in the air. Suddenly I grabbed him—I could not do otherwise—and shoved him away from the window.

But in doing so, I myself came to be standing in the window.

As I stood there, illuminated by the torches whose weak light shone up from below, as I looked down at all the pale figures who had suddenly paused in their dancing, as I leaned forward into the cool night air rising from the garden, so that my head was out under the infinite vault of heaven, I felt I had to tell them what was in my heart. I had to express myself—I could not do otherwise. Just as a short time earlier Kzradock had given voice through his mute actions, I felt I now had to try to speak out in my own way. It was as if I were continuing Kzradock's monologue; as if I followed him like another link in the same chain. I could not do otherwise.

But why?

Perhaps to master myself more completely? To test myself? Who knows? Perhaps I was still under Kzradock's influence, obeying his commands like a puppet on strings.

But there was something I hoped to learn from this, as well.

Insanity had taught the lost souls down below in the garden to dance. How would reason affect them? How would the spoken word be interpreted by these same souls? Would they become angry . . . or remain apathetic? What would happen?

I felt that my voice sounded like a struck tuning fork.

Who was I actually speaking to? To insane people and to empty rooms. And yet I could not refrain, I had to give in to my inclination. At this moment I was not merely a psychiatrist, I was a man expressing what he felt in an hour of torment.

And I spoke as loudly as I could, to be sure that everyone could understand me.

And those below were listening . . . The mad crowd listened to the open window from which they had received their orders on this strange night where everything human had come together.

"Brothers!" I said. "Dear brothers! My friends, I love you! You are fearful, you are timid, and you obeyed . . . You had no wish to do evil. Your minds have betrayed you, as has my own! And yet, in the end, what we do depends on neither our minds nor even on our souls. Our innermost mission lies outside ourselves. We all serve greater powers, both those of us who are in possession of our reason, and those who have lost it. We all must obey. We must obey and grow, grow like a plant, sprout blossoms and fruit; we must obey nature—that is the deepest drive in all of us. Brothers, how I love you! And that's why I'm speaking to you now!"

I looked out over the garden. The faces below were all turned up to me. They all listened, apprehensive and strangely silent. They were silent . . . they stood stiffly in their attitudes of listening, in which the inward energies are drawn up, and act corrosively to tattoo the soul.

And yet . . . would it have mattered if I had used a few more or a few less words? What did it mean that they were silent? Had they understood anything that I had told them?

But perhaps there was some secret music in my voice that stirred their hearts. Perhaps that was what they listened to. Perhaps just as Kzradock had led them to dance with his silent smile, I led them into obedience with my incomprehensible words. Or was it my actions that they understood rather than my words? And so we, Kzradock and I . . . were like two brothers who travel two different paths to the same destination and catch sight of one another from a distance . . . And I wondered: As we tried to get through to the others was it only the feeling that got through . . . and nothing else? Did nothing else matter?

The question flashed through me like lightning: Is there no difference? Is reason only disciplined insanity, an insane hallucination that has taken on form, and under whose influence we all live? Is reason a dream created by chance, made useable by necessity?

When these thoughts went through my brain, dedicated as it is to the religion of rationality, a shudder went through my body. But then I looked again at those intently listening faces down in the garden. The sight calmed me, and I began to speak again . . .

And this time I told them why I loved reason above all. To these lunatics, listening so intently in the dark, cold night, I spoke of the greatness of reason, of how it lives in every living thing. I spoke of the victory of reason here on earth, of the advancement of progress, of the great new epoch that would dawn for mankind, the coming paradise of reason. I spoke of everything that they might understand . . . if not feel in their heart.

By their silence they told me they were listening, and I went on.

I told them how mankind had had to struggle to work its way up out of the darkness of lies. How religion after religion had fallen before the light of truth and how reason had been able to shine through. I talked and I talked. In dramatic images, in colorful flourishes, flash after flash! I talked warmly, then heatedly, until I was boiling. I talked gladly, happily, intoxicatingly; humbly and victoriously. And those down below listened!

I had to make them understand me!

I had completely forgotten whom I was speaking to!

And then something dreadful happened!

Behind me I heard laughter.

First weakly, strangely distant, then louder and louder. The laughter cut through my voice, interrupted my hymn to reason. It suddenly grew very loud . . .

and excited. I tried to drown it out, to force my words through it. But to no avail . . . it exploded, cackled, screeched. In the middle of one of my most beautiful sentences I had to break off and turn around . . .

Kzradock lay on the floor . . . in convulsions, in a paroxysm of laughter. His chest rose and fell with it as if he had difficulty breathing. Insanity shone clearly in his eyes. He laughed in a mad frenzy of glee. He laughed like someone from whom everything has been taken . . . except laughter. He rolled in laughter, pushed out bubbles as if from a swamp of laughter. His laughter filled the room, precisely like a glass blower emptying his lungs to inflate a huge glass bubble . . . He shouted, he sang, he sobbed, and wept with laughter. He lay there like an indissoluble knot of muscular strength, a trigger for the release of the derisive laughter of the universe . . .

And I, who had so ecstatically championed reason . . . I felt something similar to what he felt . . . as he lay there . . . I could not do otherwise. I threw myself on this madman. He was not my patient, he was my mortal enemy, my contrary principle. I threw myself on him, seized him by the throat and squeezed, wild, merciless . . .

II

THE SPRING-FRESH METHUSELAH

VIII

TO BE OR NOT TO BE — THE F — GREEN AND RED INK
— THE OLD WOMEN — THE SWALLOWS' NESTS — TWO
SHOTS — THREE HUNDRED FATHOMS OF WATER — AM I
HIM? — THE SKELETON — METHUSELAH KZRADOCK

———

Three months have passed.

I am again sitting at my writing desk. I have just now read through the notes that I made about Kzradock the Onion Man. I must confess: I understand my months-long illness much better now. Obviously, a poison had trickled into my soul. But where did this poison come from?

Because Kzradock doesn't really exist.

There has never been a patient in my institute with this odd name. Kzradock is purely a fantasy figure, someone my sickness called into life. The moment I recovered, Kzradock died.

I have myself been mentally ill.

Now I am well, and the sun again plays cheerfully over my books. I sit and smile in the sunshine with these pages in front of me. These notes came into being during the dark night that I have come through. Kzradock is a part of myself, a shadow of the knowledge and experience I have had as a doctor. And this shadow had freed itself and raised itself menacingly before me.

I have to smile as I read through these pages full of horror and pain.

And, really, there is still so much that I don't understand! How was my mind driven to such savagery? What really happened to me? I was lost for so long in mysticism that I feel I have to know how my illness came about. Only then will I be able to guarantee that nothing like it will happen to me again.

There are some facts that I still cannot understand.

Why did I write the first half of the Kzradock manuscript in red ink, and the second half in green—two colors of ink that are not usually to be found on my writing desk?

There is this handkerchief imbued with an unusual fragrance, and I notice how my blood rushes to my temples when I smell it.

What has happened to me? No one knows where I was during those days when this drama played itself out. I was found under the Seine in one of those large air enclosures used by construction laborers working under the water. I had, thank God, a calling card with me that read, "There are clothes in another air enclosure." I myself lay stark naked in a corner of a filthy and damp metal box, and the memory of that is especially unpleasant for me . . .

It has been eight days since my own institute declared me fully recovered. I have made use of these days to investigate the mystery of my mind. But until now I have not wanted to read the manuscript. I was afraid of these pages with their cramped writing, and I obviously had good reason to be afraid . . .

On the first day in which I was once again in possession of my reason I took a journey abroad. I told no one where I was going. I simply packed my bag and went to the Gare Saint-Lazare. I took an express train past Dieppe, then immediately boarded the small steamer that travels across the channel to Brighton, the end point of my pilgrimage.

I went there to find out whether Lady Florence existed or not.

Those were strange and eventful days.

And I immediately had an odd experience on the train from Newhaven to Brighton: I saw the two old women.

They sat in a first-class compartment. They attracted my attention because they both had their faces turned to the compartment window and looked out as if suffering from some terrible fear. I noticed both had naïve, vacant expressions. One was a redhead and her face was quite lined. The other, who wore her hair in heavy black curls, had very striking, still youthful features, but her skin was so white with powder that she resembled a corpse.

As the train came into Brighton I heard a piercing scream.

I nervously rushed out of my compartment and was nearly knocked over by an excited-looking gentleman who stormed out of the two old women's compartment. He ran to the stationmaster and immediately brought him back. It seemed that one of the old women had fainted.

At that time I didn't know that I had been the cause of this scene. I immediately left the station and wandered through the narrows lanes of the small town.

A strange feeling of recognition filled me. Every street corner seemed familiar. And as I came to the promenade and saw the big open sea before me, it almost made me dizzy.

The strand along the vast shore was filled with people. Some strolled at the edge of the sea, while others lay in groups and enjoyed the mild afternoon sun. At some points the bathing carts had been moved into the water and the bathers stood in protective semicircles.

But I had nothing to do with any of this. I quickly walked the length of the promenade toward the white chalk cliffs behind the village. It was a long trip, and I was exhausted when I reached them.

I knew my destination.

It had gotten windy. A rain shower moved over the water and the air suddenly turned cold. The cold and the change of mood it prompted in me awoke the memory of an image. I suddenly recalled that I had walked here at night, battered by the wind, soaked by the rain. And I had not been alone. There had been two of us. She had walked by my side. She, the forgotten one, whom I was here to find, because of whom I had traveled here. She had pleaded with me, implored me as only she could. And when that had failed, she had threatened. Her small child's hand had lain on my shoulder, her eyes had sought mine in the darkness, and in the night she had called out a name, a name I no longer remembered, but merely by giving me the name, she had made me humble and obedient. She had taken me by the hand and I had followed her. And we had walked this way in the middle of the night . . . gone the very same way I now walked alone to look for the threads that connected my life . . .

Strangely enough, the wind that blew against me made me walk faster. A strong sulfur smell came to me from the strand and made me shudder. What would I see? I did not for a moment doubt that I would be able to find the place I sought. It was not much farther.

Where the chalk cliff was higher I found a narrow path that led down to the strand. The cliff was dangerously steep but my feet didn't slide on the hard surface. I stopped for a moment and looked around me. Then I saw a man's head appear momentarily above the rocks up where the path had begun. I later turned around several times to look back, and finally came to believe that I had been mistaken.

The strand there is very hard going, and endlessly lonely and dreary. It consists entirely of chalk and lime, and everywhere the water has washed away the softest chalk, low islands, pale and green with algae, have been left behind. You have to jump from island to island because channels of water run between them.

Progress was very laborious, and I grew hot and ran short of breath. Suddenly I stopped.

Was this it? I looked at the cliffs that rose quite steeply over my head. A little further on I discovered a small black cavity, and next to it two, three more small openings.

"These are the swallows' nests," I said to myself. "I still have a hundred paces to go."

Exhausted and full of dread, I hurried along the cliff. Farther along I finally found the place where it looked like there had been a rock fall. Again I stopped and looked up. The cliff was less steep here, and on looking more closely I discovered the small ledge that could be used to climb up.

As if from old habit, I first looked all around, and then I started to climb. I would never have tried it had I not known from the start that it could be done. When I reached the first small ledge, I stopped. That was when I discovered that I was being followed.

I saw him clearly as he tried to hide behind a chalk island. But he was unlucky this time. From above I could see all of him, his stooped, lurking figure, see how he had crouched down, how he had taken off his hat and now held it in his hand. Was I being watched? Who was spying on me? I tried to catch the man's eye, but he acted as if he didn't see me, and tried to give the appearance of being interested only in the snails and hermit crabs in the water at his feet.

There remained nothing for me to do but to descend once again. I had to know who was following me. Carefully and with difficulty, I climbed down an uncleared trail. Suddenly I heard a revolver shot and saw the rock five or six meters in front of me get hit. I nearly let go of the cliff, but then held on tightly as I turned my deathly pale face toward the stranger. Once again I heard a shot, and once more I heard the slapping sound of a bullet hitting the cliff. I lost my hold and tumbled downward.

Apart from a few thumps and jolts that made themselves known by the scratches they inflicted, I survived the fall in surprisingly good shape. Still, I lay there a moment, stunned, and when I raised myself up again the stranger had vanished. I set off for the spot where he had been. I walked all the way back down the small path. But the man was not to be found. I stood for a moment, uncertain. Should I return to Brighton without having learned anything? Or should I immediately try again to reach my destination? I decided to return to what I had been prevented from doing. Let things happen as they might; my trip could not be in vain. I had to know what powers had conspired against me, because not only the balance of my soul but also my ultimate fate depended upon it. For an hour I wandered on the strand in a strangely dejected but also truly excited mood. It occurred to me that the stranger resembled the man I had seen at the train station in Brighton in the company of the two old women. That realization did nothing to calm my nerves.

At last I resolved to climb the cliff again. If I had foreseen that there was another way into the cave, I would not have taken it. But I felt that an attacker could scarcely do anything to harm me if I were the first one to the top. It was discomfiting to think that I had no weapon, neither revolver nor knife, to use to defend myself. I had undertaken this trip as a peaceful traveler who would only need to fight against his memories. To feel a little more secure, I pried two flints loose from the chalk and put them in my pocket.

Thus equipped I set off on the expedition which was to become the most dangerous of my life. Still, what was all this compared to the mental suffering that I had undergone? Physical suffering is easier to bear than psychological.

Then I began again to climb the cliff. Driven by the threat of the stranger's return, I gained the first ledge relatively quickly, and remained there looking around me . . . At that moment every dark spot on the pale, deserted strand made me shudder. Could there be someone there? But everything remained quiet and still, and only the faint sounds of the ocean reached my ears.

Then I decided to climb higher.

The cave was on the next ledge. But to reach it one had first to move to the left. I have to say that as I crossed over to it I felt the needles of the fear of death. I thought, My unknown enemy is standing below me on the strand, aiming, now firing. I was already surprised that I had been able to come so far. And when I finally set foot on the ledge in front of the cave and felt I was safe at last, I completely collapsed.

When I opened my eyes again I saw that someone had written "300 fathoms of water" in black chalk on the white chalk face over the entrance to the cave.

Hadn't these same words appeared in my manuscript? Hadn't Yvonne screamed them during the murders in the Rue de Vaugirard? Yes, absolutely: the concierge had heard those very words shouted as she stood at the studio door: "There are 300 fathoms of water . . . No, no, it's no use . . . there are 300 fathoms of water."

I stared at these letters, which were also lodged in my memory. And I spoke the names Alice and Yvonne. And I suddenly saw in my memory a large yellow animal—the yellow puma. But why should I worry about it just then? Kzradock had experienced that, it had been

Kzradock who had been filled with those images. But, no! Kzradock and I were one and the same. He had lived in me and perhaps had done things I knew absolutely nothing about . . . Wasn't that right? Or was Kzradock another person, after all? And, then again, was I truly Dr. Renard de Montpensier? Was I a quiet scholar who rose every morning and spent quiet day after quiet day, week after week, in my mental hospital? Or was I one of the victims of insanity, a patient who has committed one crime after another, who has left behind a trail of bloody deeds?

Here I was, near Brighton, cowering in front of a chalk cave, over the entrance of which is written "300 fathoms of water." Did this fit Dr. Renard de Montpensier? Or was it Kzradock who lay here? And then again— what did I want here? What is hiding in this cave? Why did I come here? With what experiences would I be enriched if I returned again to the small resort town of Brighton, with its fashionable residences of Londoners who come for the summer season?

I rose with difficulty and approached the entrance. It was very confined and I had to creep in.

I noticed that the air in the cave was exceptionally dry, not damp as in the other cliff caves I knew of. As I had now recovered myself a little, I explored the low, deep cave. I felt my way forward and reached the back wall, where an old fishnet with wooden weights was hanging.

I pulled the net to one side, and the entrance to a new cave appeared.—I must have known that it existed, otherwise I would not have found it in the darkness.

The entrance to this second cave was blocked with a cloth, which I removed only with much effort because it was tangled in another fishnet. I passed through a narrow opening and finally reached the second cave, which was bigger than the first and strangely well lit. But hardly had I stuck my head in the cave when I pulled it back out, startled. In the middle of the floor lay a skeleton with raised knees and outstretched arms.

I felt a horror that I can't describe. I remained in the opening between the two caves, with my eyes fixed on these human remains. Despite my horror, the thought came to me that I had been here once before, and this sight was not as new to me as my feeling led me to believe.

I thought: If I were Kzradock . . . then I might have had something to do with what had happened here.

It reassured me and at the same time made me shudder, and so a double feeling was awakened in me, like nothing I'd ever felt before.

I finally got my courage up and I crept forward: I approached the skeleton. I believe I approached it with closed eyes. As I drew near, I saw that laid over the trunk of the skeleton was a large piece of gray cardboard with an inscription.

I raised my head and read it.

A feeling of jubilation went through me. My heart beat with violent thumps. The blood flowed into my cheeks and I sighed a sigh of pleasure. Because there on the cardboard, written in huge letters, was this: *Methuselah Kzradock*. Yes, *Methuselah Kzradock*.

But if these were Kzradock's earthly remains, and I could therefore certainly not be Kzradock, then who was I?

At this moment I was close to losing my mind completely . . .

The feeling lasted only a short time, because I suddenly heard something creeping up on me from the opposite side of the cave. I was clearly not alone in this gallery of horrors.

And now I knew how much was at stake . . .

IX

THE DEAF-MUTE DOG — BLOODLUST — HANDCUFFS —
MR. WELLS — THREE KZRADOCKS — THE GOLDEN TOOTH
— THE MUSIC OF THE SPHERES — THE GHOST CHILD —
MOTHER AND FATHER

———————

My life was at stake.

The creeping sounds that I heard came closer. Only a four-footed animal could produce such sounds. A moment later a massive bulldog jumped toward me. It was completely white, its teeth shone, and its eyes were staring directly at me. Its muscular neck tensed as if it were about to leap; it foamed at the mouth in rage.

I knew that I was finished. Because this was the deaf-mute dog. I remembered suddenly that I knew this animal, but there was no use in calling to or trying to speak to it. It could neither hear nor bark. The dog was deaf and dumb—dumb as vengeance, deaf as horror. But he wasn't blind. His big bulging eyes stared at me with furious, aggressive passion. His muteness and deafness made him doubly brutal: I would never be able to get this dog, who had no name because he could not hear it, to obey me.

I lay there without moving, my eyes nearly bursting with fear.

A moment later the dog jumped at me. He knocked me over so that I was lying on my back, and he stood on my chest. I felt his hot breath on my face. Where would he sink his teeth?

I lay that way for a long while . . . and nothing more happened. Then I risked opening my eyes a bit. To my boundless astonishment I saw that his jaws were open and that in his maw there was the white knob of a bone, and a chain that was threaded through it went around his neck and held it firmly in place. The dog's breathing was raspy with the difficulty the constriction caused him, but despite his inability to act, his wild eyes bored into mine with bitter, determined bloodlust.

I lay that way for a while, under guard. Then I suddenly heard steps from the part of the cave that I had come through. And a moment later a man ducked out from the low passageway . . . of course it was the man whom I had seen on the strand, my mysterious pursuer.

The dog became restless when it heard the steps behind him, then jumped on the new arrival with obvious delight. And the man stroked the animal without speaking to him, then took a small key out of his pocket, removed the bone, and, using hand gestures, ordered him to lie down. He put the bone in his pants pocket, but kept the key in his hand.

Then he approached me. As he stood next to me he tore off the beard that framed his face . . . he also removed his moustache and took a wig off his head . . .

"Mr. Wells!" I shouted, recognizing his red hair that suddenly lit up in the cave.

The American detective had changed quite a bit since the last time I had seen him: he had become thinner, and his features were more pronounced than before; his eyes were now screwed up and looked like two small lines in his pale face.

"Success at last," he said. "Success at last!"

And as he took a pair of handcuffs from his pocket he shouted so loud that even the deaf dog must have felt some vibration: "You are my prisoner, Dr. Renard de Montpensier! I have hunted you for a long time, because you are Kzradock!"

The bad luck my American friend had suffered during the earlier footrace suddenly came back to me. And while that had nothing to do with the present situation, I had to laugh, thinking of Mr. Wells in that embarrassing situation.

"You believe, Mr. Wells . . ." I spoke slowly and earnestly and, like a theologian, emphasized words that should not have been emphasized. "You believe I am Kzradock. A short time ago I believed it myself. I traveled to Brighton because I believed it. With that same conviction I let you shoot at me. I want to say something to you, Mr. Wells: I would be delighted to let myself be arrested, if only to bring an end to my sufferings. I would happily take upon myself all the crimes which Kzradock is said to have committed, in part due to his nature, and in part in obedience to a clandestine order that he received here at this spot, this exact spot . . . This much I know! But, just look around this cave. There beside you you will find an outstretched skeleton, and on the chest of this skeleton you will find a sign whose inscription you will easily be able to decipher, because it is written in big Latin letters. This sign has cast irrefutable doubt into my soul because it states that in life this skeleton had belonged to Kzradock. As you can see, Mr. Wells, I am still in possession of my skeleton . . . That which lies there could never have belonged to me. You want to arrest Kzradock. At this moment, detective, you are face to face with no fewer than three Kzadocks: the well, the ill, and the dead Kzradock. Which of these three is the real Onion Man?"

Mr. Wells, who had been examining the skeleton during my long speech, shook his head and said, "Have I really failed again? Or did you, Dr. Renard de Montpensier, bring this sign with you and lay it on the skeleton?"

"You would be right to be suspicious," I replied, "if you had not watched me climb the cliff, fall, and then climb it again. How was I able to transport this sign without damaging it? And you can see for yourself that it is covered with dust, and that the letters are faded! No, even if I myself wished to believe that I had brought the sign here . . . that could not have happened. And so I have to deny it categorically."

"What is the truth, and what are the lies in this damned business?" cried Mr. Wells. He looked intently at the deaf and dumb dog . . . "Again and again I have built up skyscrapers and castles of thought in attempts to clear up this mystery, and every time they have collapsed. I have nearly gone mad trying to solve this, but I can find no solution. Maybe the answer will turn out to be that I am Kzradock, although we already have three of him."

"I believe myself to be a fourth . . ." I threw in.

"But where did this skeleton come from? We apparently have here a new crime with an old date. The Kzradock who lies here is certainly not spring-fresh. But he was a man in the prime of his life, with no signs of decline. As you can see, he still had all thirty-two of his teeth. He cared for them well; there is only a single gold filling. I will have the gold analyzed. Its particular alloy may put us on the right path."

"But how did you come to be here with me in this cave?"

"The two old women put me on your trail," replied Mr. Wells. "The deaf-mute dog belongs to them. They told me how to secure the bone in his mouth, and they drew me a map of how to get here. The dog came in through a narrow entrance that lies higher up on the cliffside."

I was worried and shaking my head. "But tell me, Mr. Wells, why have you not arrested these two old women who seem to know so much about this?"

"I cannot reveal my reasons," replied Mr. Wells. "But tell me . . . what did you want in this cave? And how do you know of my acquaintance with them?"

"Well," I murmured, "I am here for the same reason you are, Mr. Wells, to find the solution to a riddle. And there lies Kzradock, and I am just as far from a solution as I was before I came . . . Who is playing with us in such a riddling way? I know that I have been in this cave before, and that dreadful things have happened here. And I also believe in my innermost soul that I am innocent . . . whether I am Kzradock or not. If you want to arrest me, Mr. Wells, then do so . . . But don't be satisfied with the explanation that the two old women or even I give you, because the truth lies elsewhere. It is as if the truth has freed itself of the body and the consciousness that it belongs to, as if it hangs right above us, like a monkey, but we are only allowed to see the tip of its tail."

Mr. Wells was suddenly as pale as death, his hands shook, and a cold sweat trickled down his brow.

"Shhh!" he whispered, and at the same time he laid his hand on my arm and stared into space as if dazed . . .

And then he whispered, "There . . . do you hear?"

I listened, but at first I heard nothing. I watched Mr. Wells and was amazed by his expression. He was submerged in a strange Nirvana-like state in which all his muscles went limp but his eyes were still alert. Even in the dim light I could see how restless his pupils were. He now turned toward me, hypnotizing me, slowing my thoughts. He was an eerie sight, and I looked away. As soon as I did I immediately understood that he was trying to gain power over me. Just then I sighted the deaf-mute dog and it, I swear, looked as if he were curiously listening to something. His round eyes stared up toward the roof as if, while deaf to all sounds in this world, he were listening to the sweet music of the spheres.

At this sight I surrendered . . . I lay down on the floor and stared up at the roof of the cave.

And I immediately heard, as if it were coming from a great distance, a delicate silvery sound like a mosquito might produce on a stormy summer night.

It was one of those sounds that fill the ear, yet was so infinitely delicate that I had to strain to hear it. The sound swelled up, gradually becoming louder, without ever losing its silvery quality. The sound became a children's song which grew softly under the roof of the cave, then nearly died away. The sound was like that of a child singing.

Then I saw that Mr. Wells had stretched out both of his arms toward the roof of the cave. He looked as if a wave of sensual ecstasy were passing through his body.

He looked like a tree, solid and yet swaying. He appeared to be swaying as a result of the storm of emotions he was feeling inside. This practical American was deep in thrall to the sound and showed no signs of resistance.

The hardnosed detective caught up in religious ecstasy was a comical sight. But I didn't laugh. I listened, completely astonished . . .

"Listen to the ghost child!" whispered Mr. Wells. "Listen to how a child's thought, freed from being tied to either gender, expresses itself! Listen to the way it sings! No earthly melody can compete! This is the song of the angels that we all dreamed of in childhood, the sound of a soul in perfect harmony!

The song truly did sound beautiful. It rose and became stronger and stronger. The voice was a delicate, lovely soprano, a clear child's voice, full of innocence and spirit. And the curious thing was that the voice moved about the cave, as if it were playing. One moment it was here, the next moment there, as if it hid from us and then revealed itself again.

Suddenly something laughed.

The voice fell silent, or more accurately, it changed into laughter, bright and cheery sounding, like a message from life itself in this cave of the dead. The laugh of a child when it awakens in the morning and opens its eyes; a happy child without worries . . .

"Ow, ow!" It was Mr. Wells. He shouted and tugged at his hair.

"What is it?" I asked.

"It pulled my hair. Look . . . Look!"

I saw nothing, but I thought I felt the touch of a hand that lay on my forehead and stroked my cheeks and in the end teased me by pulling on my beard. I tried to seize the invisible one that was touching me, and thought I felt something slip between my fingers. It was more a cold than a warm sensation . . . the sensation of touching a glass of cold water in a warm room. I experienced that image so strongly that I simultaneously felt a burning thirst.

All at once, the deaf-mute dog began to stir. He jumped up, struggled with something in mid-air, stood on his hind legs, and tried to bark. But while the laughter was audible all round, where the dog itself jumped, there was no sound. He danced around and butted his head against the air as if into something solid.

Some moments passed in which everything was quiet. The singing and laughter had stopped, and we felt embarrassed, as if we had been cheated, fooled by something. But then we suddenly heard a child's voice which shouted, "Mother is coming . . . Mother is coming . . ."

At that point I recalled how Lady Florence had always wished to have a child, a child not of flesh and blood but of soul and spirit, a child whose mission was the free unfolding of thought, and whose sphere of action would range from the aether up to seventh heaven.

Was it Lady Florence's child who floated over our heads, happily playing, innocently singing? Ever more joyfully its voice rang out from the roof of the cave: "Mother is coming! Mother is coming!" And when steps could be heard coming from the cave entrance the deaf-mute dog had earlier come through, the invisible floating child of the new arrival cried out in its clear soprano, "Father is here . . ! Father is here . . !"

X

———————

Lady Florence stood in the cave. I recognized her the moment I saw her. How could I have done otherwise?

It was as if everything outside the cave had fallen away in the distance. I saw only her, while time and space vanished. How beautiful she looked! Like a young girl . . . a child that must be held . . . a youth from the morning of time, with an unspoiled sparkle in her eyes.

But she really wasn't young, and that could be seen as well. She only seemed young. But she also looked like an old woman, with the beauty of wisdom and experience that created an exceptional translucency . . . It was as if all stages of life and death could simultaneously be seen in her features. The apeman and the superman, the rise of the sexes on the evolutionary ladder, were reflected in her eyes . . . Oh yes, she resembled every man's dream, an eternal presence that rose, rung by rung, toward an always new and perfect beauty.

How did she look?

She was tall, slim, and brunette, boyish in her slimness, changeable, as if filled with a mysterious nerve-fire. Everything about her, her black hair and depthless pallor, showed spirit, as did the blending of tenderness and cruelty around her mouth, and her slim hands with their abnormal, ape-like nails. She looked like she belonged more to death than life, looked like a dream, an adulteress, a criminal . . .

I saw only her . . . and felt that she had the same power over my soul that she had had in the past. Who was I? Was I Renard de Montpensier, chief doctor of an insane asylum in Paris? No, certainly not. Was I Kzradock? Certainly not Kzradock, who, sick and haunted, led a phantom existence in a world of delusions and deceptions. I suddenly felt very young, filled with a zest for life and with warmth, recklessly in love with no one in particular! My blood flowed freely through my veins; I felt as if my hair now fell in waves. I was spring fresh . . . who was I, really? Methuselah? Was I the spring-fresh Methuselah?

But if I was, then I might also be Kzradock, who lay here as a skeleton. Hadn't the sign read, "Methuselah Kzradock"?

Then I suddenly heard Lady Florence's voice.

"Too soon," she whispered softly, silkily. "Too soon! Why can't romance last forever? Why can no human mind bear the burden that nature imposes upon it? Fate has not favored me. My will has not been able to accomplish what I wished. What should have become truth has become only lies . . ."

I could not refrain . . . I could not help myself. I called to her in a voice that in my ears sounded like that of a trembling old man: "I am still young, Lady Florence!"

"That's not true . . ." she answered. "Were you not ordered seven times to speak, and did you not struggle like a lion against my will? Have you not become mentally ill and gray-haired, have you not become the chief doctor of an insane asylum, all merely to defy my orders? And you call yourself young? Where is the ring I gave you? Where are you yourself? I gave you my power, and you have used it to create confusion and doubt. But that's all over now! The child, the one we should have had together, is only a hallucination. The reality is the anatomical exhibit that lies here. Even my happy dog is a deaf-mute."

She pointed at the skeleton.

"There lies the reality," she cried. "The reality is a crime . . . Just as I wanted it to be. What Yvonne and Alice did not foresee before their murder in the Rue Vaugirard I believe I understand. But before I die you should know who could tell you how all this came to be. The two old women have the answers. They have Ulysse Vanil locked away in a garret. For company they have given him an old cat that in the evening sits in the attic window and with its round eyes looks up at the moon. The cat is so clever that he can speak some human words.

Listen carefully to what he says, it is important . . . And now, farewell!"

She raised her arms to the roof of the cave and pressed something invisible there. At that moment Mr. Wells grabbed her. He had seen a dagger flash. He grabbed her wrist and held it tight.

"Lady Florence, I arrest you in the name of the law," he shouted. "You believe that you can withdraw with impunity from this mysterious affair. But I hereby charge you of being guilty of murder, burglary, and hypnotic influence. Help me, Dr. Renard de Montpensier, help me. Hold her hands while I handcuff her. She is as strong as the Goddess of Insanity herself."

I was standing next to Mr. Wells. Lady Florence stomped three times on the floor of the cave and the deaf-mute dog instantly ran to attack us. He threw himself on Mr. Wells and dragged him down so that he fell across the skeleton. He opened his warm maw over the throat of the man lying on the ground, waiting only for his mistress's command to sink his teeth into it.

But the command didn't come. Lady Florence stood for a long moment and looked down at Mr. Wells. Then she said, "I shall not die just yet. He deserves to learn the truth. How painful it would be for him. He would die of laughter if he knew! But we will take care of him, we will put the handcuffs on him; have him experience the feel of the cold iron that he intended for me. I will grant this to this American detective! See how red his hair blazes! Like blood! In America I learned from an old Indian how his forefathers scalped their enemies. I have not had the opportunity to make use of my knowledge in this regard . . . until now! I will take his red scalp. This will be my last good deed in this world. I will scalp him!"

"In God's name," I said, "don't do that! That would only add a new crime to all the others . . ."

"Not at all," retorted Lady Florence. "What do these people seek and sniff out? What should we do with this idiotic detective who writes thick detective novels and spurs on the fantasies of his public in such an insane fashion? I value the idea that our privacy is sacred; he violates it. Since Sampson's time it has been said that a man's strength resides in his hair. That must hold true for detectives, as well. So we should scalp them whenever the opportunity presents itself . . . Go on!"

I heard a plaintive sound coming from the air. Was the spirit child crying? Could it not bear to see blood? I didn't know, but perhaps that was the case. Because when Lady Florence raised the dagger she pushed something invisible aside with her free hand. She bent down and with a quick, violent, and ruthless motion made a circular incision. I heard Mr. Wells groan and wail and scream a hideous scream as Lady Florence grasped his red hair with both of her hands and stripped his scalp from his head. It was a terrible moment, and I went pale and my knees began to tremble. I nearly fainted when I saw the red mat of hair come loose in Lady Florence's hand.

"That was a nasty job," she said, balancing lightly on her slim legs, "but it was a success! Now we will give the detective's scalp to the deaf-mute dog!"

With that she dropped the scalp on the ground and nudged it toward the dog. The monster flung himself on the scalp with determined fury and consumed every bit of skin and hair so that not the slightest trace of it remained. He had barely finished swallowing the last bite when he began sniffing around, as if there were something there to discover. The scalp had obviously excited his bloodlust.

For her part, Lady Florence laughed at the sight. With an expression of complete indifference, she looked at how blood had mixed with tears on Mr. Wells's cheeks while he rattled the handcuffs to try to get her attention. She stood there as if sunk in deep thought. She suddenly ran her hands through her hair, freed it, and let it fall over her shoulders in a dark, melancholy stream. It was so heavy and thick that it covered her face like a cowl. She pushed it back and said, "Do you remember? What night that was . . . ? Tell me if you still remember!"

She leaned toward me and her hair touched my cheek. And, as before, I felt spring-fresh and young, happily playing with this young woman and with my fate.

In the midst of all her dark hair I saw her red mouth, strangely tempting and seductive. And I moaned.

"It was the night of the third and fourth of May."

"You still remember?"

"Yes."

"It was our wedding night."

"It was the same night in which . . . oh, do you still recall the horrors . . . as in the morning on the Rue de Vaugirard the police crowded in, and Alice and Yvonne lay stretched out on the floor . . . Alice dying first, her throat cut. A horrible night . . . and that was our wedding night, Florence."

"Yes," whispered Lady Florence, "my lover. And now our child is three years old."

"Our child?"

"Yes, our poor child . . . have you never thought about our child? Have you forgotten that it was the result of our struggle, this poor nothing which others would only smile at, but for me is terribly serious? Why have you not obeyed me, and remained in your dream? Now I am willing to answer you if you ask what has come from all the risks and unpleasantness that I have gone through; what my soul created when it found yours . . . You will have to seek the answer to the larger riddle elsewhere, but I can show you the result of our encounter. I will show you our child . . . but it will cost me the last of my strength. Now look . . . listen and look!"

She covered my head with her hair. I felt it sweep over me like a wing, and felt her skin and her hair. Then everything grew still and a deep feeling of well-being came over me, and I closed my eyes. When I opened them again, a small child was standing at her feet, a small three-year-old who looked with big innocent eyes into my own.

"Is it a boy?" I whispered.

"Of course it's a boy," she answered. "Can't you see that? He is the child of our love. And this is the last time I will ever see him. Look at his innocent eyes—how they resemble your own! Don't you want to hold him in your arms? Don't you want to play with him for a moment?"

"What's his name?"

"His name is Renard."

"Really?"

"Renard! He is named after his father, Renard de Montpensier . . . Isn't that true, isn't your name Renard?" she asked the boy.

"Of course," he answered.

I was startled. "But then I once again don't understand a thing . . . Am I now Renard de Montpensier, or am I Kzradock?"

I was suddenly suspicious, and I asked, "Is or isn't this my son?"

Lady Florence shook her head and answered sullenly. "I certainly hope so! But I am not completely sure. And now you shall hear . . ."

I was angrier than I had ever been. I felt heat climbing up my body and into my brain, and I was nearly boiling with rage as I cried, "You don't know? You don't know whether this is the child of our love? And you might not even know who I am? You don't know whether I am Kzradock or Renard de Montpensier, or even a third or a fourth man? You are merely trying to find a father for your ghost child. We once spent many happy hours together. But everything that followed has been unhappiness and insanity. You have made me an onion, a Methuselah, a Kzradock. Must I now ask who I am and why I am here? You have made me a criminal and a mass murderer, you have locked me in a madman's cell. I would have given everything for our love. But I will not be a father to a ghost child who belongs to another. In these romantic moments, where everyone is either a criminal or a detective, many things can happen. But this, my dear, is too much. And now I want to know who I am, who you are, and what sense there is in all of this. It means our lives, even our everlasting salvation. I want to leave this hellhole, where everything is murder and madness, and go out into God's nature, where the sun is shining. But tell me first, who am I? Who in the devil's name am I?"

There was a pause and I heard the boy at our feet cry out, "Father! Mother! Why are you arguing?"

I gave the little devil a slap, and he began to cry loudly, to blubber so hard that he couldn't catch his breath.

Only when I had struck the boy's head a sufficient number of times did he become silent, and invisible.

As you might imagine, Lady Florence was furious. She raged like a fury, pulled out the dagger and stabbed out blindly to her right and to her left. At the last moment she cried, "You want to know who you are . . . You think I know, you old idiot! And what concern is that of mine, anyway? You will have to ask about yourself somewhere else . . . I am Lady Florence and now I am leaving this tragic scene. You can try to find the two old women, and from them you will learn the whole truth. But watch out for their eyes! . . . I no longer wish to live. You have bit by bit made a complete fool of me . . . What I had achieved, you have destroyed. It is time that I lay down my magic wand. Of what use was it to take the detective's scalp, if I am still left with you? God knows you begin to bore the public, which demands more murders and mystifications than I can manage with only your help . . . No, I want no more of it. I will die and leave you behind with a ghost child, a scalped detective, a skeleton and a deaf-mute dog. It is enough for you to handle. I wish you a happy life!"

With that, Lady Florence thrust the dagger into her heart and fell to the ground. She was dead. A shudder still goes through me when I remember how she looked . . . Had I really dedicated my life to her? Oh, you gods!

XI

WHISKEY AND SQUAB — THE KEY — THE TAPEWORM —
WALLET AND PURSE — SHOTS — THE DAUGHTER OF
TWO MOTHERS — THE LOCKED-AWAY — METHUSELAH
KZRADOCK — THE FISHING LINE

———

I had few remaining illusions when I left the cave, and I was no doubt a fairly comic figure as I walked along the strand, my hat pulled down in shame over my eyes. At that moment, I had no idea where to turn. Everything seemed trivial, and I was like a Robinson Crusoe stranded on the island of Absurdity, with only a ghost child, a scalped detective, a skeleton, and a deaf-mute dog for company. What a collection of oddities in solitude!

I looked out over the ocean that foamed and strained against its bonds like a captive Prometheus. I looked at the sky, which was blank and empty.

I suddenly saw a small boy coming toward me. He handed me a piece of paper and went on his way. I unfolded the paper and read,

*The undersigned, who every evening prays for the life
of his customers, has opened an elegantly appointed*

wine cellar on the corner of Victoria and Albert Street.
You only need pay me a visit and you will thereafter be
included in my evening prayers.

Respectfully yours,
Dick Hardy

P.S. Our whiskey springs from paradise, and our squab
from the ark.

I read the note through twice, and an easy smile
played over my lips. Why not go, I thought. After all, I
have to eat something after all this unpleasantness.

When I arrived at Victoria Street, the proprietor
was standing in the door. He was obviously quite surprised to see a customer at this hour of the day. It turned
out that his restaurant was a rather dubious bar, dirty
and disorderly. I ordered a portion of the squab that
came from the ark, but I discovered that it wasn't served
until evening.

Still feeling desperate, I settled in and had a whiskey.

My host had a drink, too. He was clearly watching
me. He didn't let me out of his sight for a moment. He
appeared to be up to something. I had the feeling that he
would try to get me drunk, then attack and rob me.

After a time he stood up, went to the door, and
turned the key. In my half-tipsy state I watched as he approached and stood in front of me.

"Give me your watch," he ordered. "Your wallet and your coin purse . . . I'll be content with that."

I felt I had no alternative and would have to comply. I handed him my gold watch. But hardly was it in his hand when he fell to the floor unconscious.

What is this? I wondered. Has the man gone insane? It was my opportunity to make my escape. I bent down to retrieve my watch and noticed that its cover had opened, and that the hands stood at 4:15.

I seized my watch and ran to the door, turned the key, and would have gone straight out except that the owner moved. Still only half-conscious, he murmured, "Is it really so late?"

I stopped short and stood still for a moment. I knew I could flee whenever I wished. I watched as the man rose and squinted toward me, and then he cried out, "That damned tapeworm!"

"What do you mean?" I laughed scornfully. "First you distribute religious tracts. Then you try to clean me out. Then you have an epileptic fit, and now you curse your tapeworm as if had something to do with this business. What are you talking about?"

"Oh," he answered, rubbing his eyes, "it all goes together. The tapeworm is to blame for everything. He rules me; I am completely in his power. He is my inner mainspring for good and evil. If he is wound gently, I feel religious. When he is fidgety, I feel the desire to commit terrible crimes. And after four o'clock, when my lunch has reached my colon, there always comes a moment when he thrashes around savagely, and then I fall down as if dead."

"That is certainly a beautiful excuse," I said. "But it was good that he fidgeted . . . otherwise you would have stolen my watch, my coin purse, and my wallet."

"You'll have to forgive me," said the proprietor, "but he was very hungry today. Because it has been more than twenty-four hours since I last ate my midday meal, and he has not had food nor drink since then. Usually the dear beast understands me, but under such unusual circumstances it incessantly asks what is wrong, and it asks in extremely disagreeable ways!"

"You should get rid of the beast," I said, and I turned to leave.

"Listen a moment," cried the owner. "No, he should stay where he is. He provides me with change and appetite. Fourteen times a day he makes a new man out of me. Even last night as I wandered about among the chalk rocks he entertained me." I suddenly became interested in the man's story.

"What were you doing last night among the chalk rocks?"

"I was keeping watch."

"Watch?"

"Yes, I was stationed there, close to Brighton, and to await some shots, but they never came. Or maybe I didn't hear them over the inner uproar my tapeworm was making."

I listened intently, my hand still on the door handle. And I tried to keep calm as I asked him, "Some shots, you say?"

"Yes, two old women sent me out there. Do you know those two strange broads? They live in the house opposite. Last night they waited up for me. When I came home early this morning their light was still burning and they immediately came over and asked me to go out again. I only got back an hour ago."

I moved closer to him.

"Will the tapeworm allow me to sit for a moment?"

"Sure," he replied. "I'm not dangerous right now. Would you like another whiskey?"

I sat at the table next to the door. I had hidden the key, and so felt safe in taking him up on his offer.

"They must be interesting women," I said. "How long have they lived here?"

"As long as I can remember," he answered. "They are both old. But they have a daughter."

"Both of them?"

"Yes, they are both the mother of their one daughter."

"Go to the devil!"

"It's absolutely true," he replied. "They told me all about it. It seems that they both had a child at the same time. One daughter died and they no longer remember whose child died."

"What is the daughter's name?"

"Her name is Florence."

I turned pale. Fortunately the owner didn't notice. He was staring at the house opposite as if he expected an order to come from there. He stared steadily out the window.

I had time to regain my composure.

"And Florence lives with her mothers?"

"Yes, she has been living there recently. She is quite an odd girl. If you only knew . . ."

I looked out, as if I knew nothing. But I also could not avoid staring over at the house opposite, a pretty three-story building with many windows. In the uppermost window, the attic window, sat a huge cat, which pressed its body tightly against the windowpane and licked one of its paws.

"The house looks so quiet," the owner said. "But over there all kinds of things go on. If I only had more information . . ."

He leaned toward me and whispered, "I want to tell you what I do know. Do you see that small attic window? Behind it sits a man, locked away. I also know that he is forbidden to go near the window. But sometimes I still see his pale face, and sometimes he gives me a sign . . ."

"A sign that you should go to his aid?"

"No, it's always the same sign. He raises both hands and shows me his ten fingers. Then he closes and opens his hands twice, and lastly he shows me only two fingers. In total, he shows me thirty-two fingers. Thirty-two . . ."

"What does he mean?"

"Well, I've never had the chance to ask him about it. Now and then I hear him play his flute—in fact he always plays the same note; he repeats one note six times."

"Strange!" I said.

"Everything in that house is strange. I have never been above the first floor. But what I have seen on the stairs and in the rooms on the first floor was all extremely odd. The rooms are filled with painted scenery as for a theater, and there are electric wires and water pipes in the strangest places. And now I want to tell you something that will astonish you . . . All the steps on the stairs are loose . . . I always have the feeling that I am walking over a pit when I have to go up them . . ."

I looked at him and he looked at me. We both shook our heads.

"But didn't you tell me just now," I asked, "that you help the old women now and then?"

"Certainly," he replied. "And that, by God, is the strangest thing of all. They use me to do their spying. I was to go to the rocks and wait for shots and signals. But I never heard the right signal."

"Wasn't there a shot fired out there this morning?"

"How do you know that?"

"I was out that way . . . I heard it."

"It was surely Mr. Wells who fired that shot," said the owner. "But it was not the signal I was waiting for."

"Do you know Mr. Wells?"

"He is my brother."

"Really!" I said. "Now I begin to understand . . ."

"What are you beginning to understand? Who are you? Are you perhaps the movie theater manager that those across there have been expecting?"

I know my face showed my incomprehension. But I could not do otherwise. As I stared fixedly at the owner I said, "Three hundred fathoms of water . . ."

He suddenly rose up, grabbed me by the shoulder and cried, "Where is Lady Florence?"

"She is dead," I answered, and I grabbed a chair and put it between the owner and me, and I simultaneously began my retreat toward the door.

But to my great surprise the owner cried out, "Thank God!" And immediately after that, "Still, what will they say over there?"

"Listen," I said after a short pause. "Do you know a man named Renard de Montpensier?"

"No."

"Then do you know someone named Methuselah?"

I was as white as a sheet with tension and fear.

"That was my name in the old days," answered the owner.

"What was your name?"

"My name was Methuselah Kzradock."

Now I was the one who almost sank to the floor. I felt as if my tapeworm had begun to stir. But by this time I was so used to surprises that I only said, "Could you repeat that? Your name is Methuselah Kzradock?"

And when the bar owner nodded, I went on, with rising agitation.

"Listen . . . we must go together over to that house. And you must promise me that you won't let me out of your sight for a second! You must stay by my side, so there will be no confusion. But, tell me first, do you have the courage to explain to those two old women over there that you are Methuselah Kzradock?"

His answer astonished me: "They already know it. Those two old women are responsible for the fact that I'm now called Dick Hardy. It's even their fault that I love my tapeworm and look after it and have been successful in seeing it as a reasonable substitute for my true love."

I put my head in my hands. "Am I the one who is insane here?"

"No," answered the bar owner. "You are not insane, but perhaps you have drunk too much whiskey. Still, it's all true."

"Let's go across now," I shouted. "I need to make some sense of this thing. I must know whether I am insane or drunk, or if I still have my five senses. Oh, even another man's tapeworm gives me pain. Promise me that you'll cross over with me at once. Where is your hat and coat? And lend me a cane, in case it should be needed . . ."

By chance, I looked out the window at just that moment and I found myself standing there as if fossilized. One of the windows on the second floor had been opened. And out of it jutted a long fishing rod with line and hook. But instead of a fish hanging on the hook there was a key ring.

"Look," said the bar owner. "They are calling me . . ."

With these words he gave my chest a shove, so that I rolled to the ground, and then he leapt into the street outside.

I quickly regained my feet, excited, wondering what would happen outside. And I walked far enough into the street that the key ring struck me on the head. It had fallen from the hook that had been swung out from inside.

The key hurt, but that didn't concern me. I and no one else now had the key ring. I was finally the master of the situation.

Master of the situation!

Now the riddle of my life and my destiny would be solved.

XII

I stood there with the key to the riddle in my hand.

I hurried to the door and put the key into the lock.

In that instant the door, house, street, earth, and sky all disappeared.

I was alone with the ghost of madness, which resembled something's shaggy breast. And I felt at that moment that the entire world had been nothing more than painted stage flats that had collapsed in on themselves at the first gust of wind, while reality was a shaggy beast that had long pursued me and now had sunk its teeth into my throat.

I felt terror; I felt my life ebbing away. And, as silence gained power over my heart, I felt a strange delight . . .

I only learned eight days later that I had been found in the Hall of Pain, found in my own asylum.

But the first thing that I learned when I recovered from my eight-day illness was this: "I am Dr. Renard de Montpensier."

And Kzradock?

As I announced quite early on in these notes, Kzradock doesn't really exist.

What I didn't know at that time, however, was that Lady Florence also belongs to the world of unreality.

The many inconsistencies in her life and fate show that conclusively—to a healthy mind.

Kzradock and everything that befell him was created by me. My madness created an entire drama around an imaginary central figure . . .

I now understand that the solution to all of these riddles can be found only within my ego, not anywhere outside it.

My illness had made me a poet. What insanity the mind of a poet must contain.

People who have never existed wake from their nothingness, and the wretches are introduced into a world where everything occurs as if by magic, in a play of forces which owe their eternity to the poet himself. And in that world nothing can be concluded before the poet's obsession has passed. He lives in the world of reality, and there is not a free man.

His poetry is his liberation.

Through it he purchases his freedom from reality and reenters the world where the sun shines and the trees are green.

Yes, it is spring once again . . .

Outside my window the acacias are blooming. They also have gone through the dream time of winter, and who knows what trees dream of.

For a blind, deaf tree, wouldn't winter be a ghost that presses down on its boughs, a Kzradock that lets terrors descend on the tree? If the storms howl and the darkness of winter surrounds it, isn't it Kzradock who wails in its crown? And isn't it Kzradock who tries to thwart its urge to rise and its vitality? And isn't it the fear of the young Methuselah that encircles the tree?

This year my soul has endured winter and a time of death.

And here is the solution to the riddle: Kzradock is insanity.

Kzradock is the fear the always locked-away soul has of itself.

The locked-away soul will murder, will commit any crime, to maintain its illusion. The locked-away soul fashions, within itself, its own opposite. If it is a man's soul, it will produce his female opposite. In this case, Lady Florence . . .

She looked like the kind of woman who would be able to dominate me!

I have seen her in my imagination, but I have not met her in reality.

Oh, Lady Florence, so surprisingly intertwined are the threads of life that you do not exist at all!

And, nevertheless, you have dominated me.

Despite your unreality you have taken me by the hand and have led me through a red sea of suffering, until I was found lying like a dead man in the Hall of Pain.

I created you, and you became my ruler. I have been in your power.

Who knows whether I have truly escaped . . .

Nevertheless, at this moment I feel free.

And now I can turn to my readers . . . Alas, my readers are as imaginary, as unreal as Kzradock and Lady Florence.

I have written all of this for myself, out of my fears of death and pain. And who knows if it will ever find other readers?

Should these pages ever come into someone else's hands, should they actually be read, and should a discussion about them arise, I believe I know what my readers' feelings would be . . .

They would feel deceived, fooled, and cheated.

As do I!

My notes have neither beginning nor end, neither head nor tail . . .

But in this very lack lies the lesson that should be taken from them.

The lesson that I myself have taken from them.

Anyone who has read these pages through to the end has gone through the sufferings of a sick soul.

They have seen how a strained soul creates an entire world within the skin that surrounds it . . .

I would wish that my readers would believe in this fantasy world, and that the experience yields them some profit, however strange. Because then they will not have been cheated, but will have gotten to know the secrets of the soul.

In that case, they will have learned a profound truth: that one should not trust one's soul. One should not trust the illusions that the soul unrolls and then only half carries through.

No one can escape the sufferings of the soul.

But you have to doubt.

You have to doubt your own soul.

If you trust it, it will free itself and gain power over your life. And it will create a domain of belief in which you will then have to live.

So those of my future readers who have most been deceived, have at the same time received the most serious warning. They have believed in Kzradock—and he was nothing . . . he was a diabolical joke, and yet he was deadly serious. He was the soul that, with closed eyes, departs from reality. He was the dark of night in the mind of man.

If I had not believed in him everything would have been different.

But who among my readers who believed in him would not feel just as cheated as I do? Who hasn't felt Methuselah Kzradock in himself? Oh, who has not? Who has not felt the eternally young, eternally old trust in the wild dreams of the soul? Who has not believed in them and sought to carry them through?

Who has doubted at the right moment?

Haven't you . . . and you . . . and you felt some obsession, and so stood at the edge of the abyss?

For those who understand this, these notes will not have been written in vain. In quiet hours, when their soul is about to lead them astray, they will remember Methuselah Kzradock.

But for those who understand nothing of this, these notes may perhaps still be a pleasant entertainment. They will be amused, or perhaps be angry—if angry they wish to be! But they will understand nothing because they haven't found Kzradock in themselves.

Such readers will take what I have written as a detective novel with no solution.

In a certain sense, this is also correct.

The soul is the best detective. But it can never find the solution to its own riddle, because this lies in itself. It can look at itself, it can believe and it can doubt.

It can do no more.

. . . Oh, the modern soul is badly in need of help and support, what with being exposed to so many temptations from both inside and outside, from religion and suggestion, from willfulness and eroticism.

And it has that help within itself.

It can doubt.

Don't believe all the tales your soul whispers to you! Don't take them at face value before you investigate further ...

And keep constant watch on your doubt; make sure that it doesn't disappear.

Because doubt is the only weapon you have against yourself.

For that matter, these notes could be read in the same way.

With doubt.

Readers who understand immediately what I learned so slowly, will have a great time at my expense. With their sure instincts they will understand what a reed in the wind I have been. They will understand that all my sufferings grew from a revolting parody of human life.

I have to appreciate such readers, because they came out of the morass before me. If I should meet them, I would show them respect and shake their hands deferentially.

May I meet many such readers!

I believe that I now understand the human onion.

Man is much more a plant than an animal. In outward appearance he has the form of an animal. But everything inside is like a plant. The outside is only an instrument; what's inside is what's important ...

The soul is like a plant that grows in accordance with the laws of its seed.

Encased in the experiences of generations, the soul can be compared to an onion with many layers of onionskin. Inside them is the seed, capable of producing life. The seed must grow in the right way if a man is to develop properly and blossom.

In the spring of youth—a time of life that, paradoxically, is determined by experiences as old as Methuselah—the onion seed grows full of confidence.

This is the time of trust.

Then come the disappointments, the collisions with reality, times of misfortune and failed hopes, and finally the breakdown, perhaps even insanity . . .

It is necessary to arm oneself with masculine pride, to, at the very least, salvage what can be salvaged. And doubt steps into the gap where trust had been.

Such is the law of growth.

And one must obey this law . . . or die!

I myself am a beaten man.

My will is broken.

But at the same time the seals on my mouth have been broken. I now understand my inner life . . . if not my outer one.

And in my defeat lies my redemption.

I want to plunge into the Gospel of Doubt and preach it to everyone who has the ears to hear.

No one should believe me.

No one should believe themselves.

Insanity, Kzradock, will perish in the face of doubt!

Doubt will grow to be the supreme power in my soul; its rule there shall be absolute.

This is my will.

I want! I want!

I want doubt!

With this wish I bring these notes on Kzradock the Onion Man to an end.

TRUST, DOUBT, AND MADNESS
ON LOUIS LEVY'S *KZRADOCK*

Louis Levy was born in Copenhagen in 1875, and died in Charlotten-lund, Denmark, in 1940. His father was a surgeon, and Levy initially planned to become a doctor. Instead he had a long career as an author, writing novels, political history, children's stories, poetry, and stage plays—including one about Hans Christian Andersen—even plays for marionettes. Levy traveled abroad and worked as a correspondent for Danish newspapers, including the *Berlingkse Tidende* and *Politiken*. He also worked in radio. In his native Denmark he is now best remembered for his collections of nursery rhymes.

Outside Denmark, Levy's works are nearly forgotten today, with only *Kzradock* and *The Truth about France*, his book about fascism in France between the world wars, having left much of a trace else-where.[1] *Menneskeløget Kzradock, den vaarfriske Methusalem: Af Dr. Renard Montpensiers Optegnelser* appeared in *Maaneds-Magasinet*, a Danish illustrated monthly in 1909, and in book form in 1910. It was translated into German as *Die Menschenzwiebel Kzradock und der*

Frühlingsfrische Methusalem in 1912 by Hermann Kiy. This was reissued in 1986. The present translation, the first into English, was made from the German translation and then kindly checked against Levy's Danish original by Annette David.

Levy was clearly familiar with Paris—not just with its geography, but with the look of its lights, with the blur of its quick changes of fashion, its teeming crowds, so vividly captured in Renard de Montpensier's comments as he rides on the top deck of a bus speeding through the streets. Levy was also familiar with Gallic resignation and various American idiosyncrasies, which he needles in several satirical asides. *Kzradock* also shows evidence of Levy having had at least a passing familiarity with the basics of psychology, sociology, biology—even the operation of steam-powered fire-fighting equipment. In short, the kind of generalist's knowledge a well-traveled journalist might acquire. There may be a touch of autodidact's mockery in Levy's creation of the pompous Dr. Renard de Montpensier (who always refers to himself by his full name and title). Rationality, as he tells his (potential) readers, is his religion. He is very much concerned with his professional dignity and his principles, and more than a little vain of his education and of his science, psychology, "which reduces all people to their basic elements."

Levy also clearly was familiar with the basic elements of the detective novel. Such novels were as popular in Denmark as they were in America. A report in the *New York Times* of 6 February 1910 tells of "Nick Carter" detective stories being given out by Danish newspapers as premiums. But *Kzradock* is also very close kin to the Gothic novel, and even to the symbolism of Mallarmé and Baudelaire, of which Levy the journalist and sometimes Paris resident would likely have been aware. Levy's use of melodramatic events (a man held prisoner in an attic; Bayle the puma, who is surely a deliberate nod to Poe's "The Murders in the Rue Morgue"), foreboding locations (a cave, a metal chamber under the Seine, a mental hospital), the cliché that perhaps Kzradock has kept the image of his attacker in his eyes, and even in his copious use of exclamation points, shows his debt to these sources.

The conceit of a possibly mad narrator allows Levy an unusually free hand in the invention of characters and incidents. But we also notice that the voice of the narrator—and, in at least one instance, one of the characters—is at times indistinguishable from what we can hear as the voice of the author, addressing the reader directly. Near the climax of the wrenching emotional struggle between de Montpensier and Lady Florence in the cave, for example, she says to him,

> . . . I am still left with you? God knows you begin to bore the public, which demands more murders and mystifications than I can manage with only your help.

And when Dick Hardy describes the house of the two old women, he could easily be describing a backstage area: "The rooms are filled with painted scenery as for a theater, and there are electric wires and water pipes in the strangest places."

Detective stories and novels proceed by frustrating expectations. What seems to be, is not; red herrings and opaque clues lead the reader to an expectation, which is then deferred to create suspense. A detective's most valuable tool is his sense of doubt. With *Kzradock* Levy takes the genre's frustration of expectation to extremes. If we look at the ways Levy manipulated the detective novel's conventions, yet another question arises: was Levy primarily interested in subverting the detective genre, or in presenting a philosophy of epistemological doubt, and simply understood the mystery tale to be the ideal form for doing so? Either way, form and idea are a perfect fit.

Among those who found the novel's insistence on the wisdom of pervasive doubt to be compelling were Walter Benjamin and Gershom Scholem. Scholem and Benjamin shared an interest in "the most important detective novels—those . . . which, at their best, are characterized by an unapproachable purity of spheres."[2] In *Kzradock* they seem to have found the apotheosis of this "purity."

On 15 April 1918, Scholem wrote in his journal that he, on Benjamin's recommendation, had just finished reading *Kzradock*.

> This is a great book, and it speaks a formidable language. "You have to doubt. You have to doubt your own soul." This book lays out the metaphysics of doubt. The terrible law by which the soul germinates, if one trusts it, is developed in this detective story without a solution. The story's beginning and end both lie in the unspeakable, in human demonism, which only doubt can overcome. The verdict of this book is legitimate and its artistic unity is morally harrowing, because it generates that unity from the law of the demonic. In fact, only doubt makes the madness in the art bearable, and the (metaphysical) anonymity of the book is critical to its idea: Trust is madness.[3]

In an undated entry, probably written in July or August of 1918, Scholem returned to the book, this time expanding his thoughts about it to make a point about his view of Judaism:

> The detective novel is the true literature of the philosophy of moral law.[4] This is why *Kzradock the Onion Man and the*

Spring-Fresh Methuselah is such a tremendous book. Every detective novel questions the foundations of moral law—none answer the questions, but they reach the highest sphere, which is doubt. "You have to have doubt. You have to doubt your own soul." Love in a real detective novel is romantic, ironic because it is affirmative. The crime springs out of love, because doubt (the "doubt of your soul") is forgotten, and out of wickedness as well, because doubt is suppressed. . . . The realization of doubt is innocence. . . . Only doubting is good. This sentence is Torah. We don't believe, only the criminal believes, because in this world only the believer affirms or denies the "realizing doubt." Doubt is justice; doubting is law. Judaism is the religion in which doubt's religious place is at the center . . . and so thereby is Judaism the religion of justice and fairness.[5]

And while Scholem was later to disavow some of his youthful interests and choices in reading, he never dismissed *Kzradock*. In his memoir *Walter Benjamin: The Story of a Friendship*, written more than a half-century later, Scholem refers to the novel yet again as a "hidden metaphysics of doubt."[6]

When Scholem read *Kzradock* he was a twenty-year-old student who had been thrown out of school and out of his father's house for anarchist activities. He was living in Switzerland, studying at a university and sweating out a draft deferment. He had moved to Switzerland in large part to be able to have daily conversations with Benjamin. Scholem was at this time consumed by two areas of study: philosophy and higher mathematics, which he had planned to make his life's work; and the Kabbalah—the then-disreputable texts of Jewish mysticism, which were ultimately to be the star he would follow.

With these seemingly contradictory interests (which Scholem nonetheless seemed to find strangely complementary, in that they both promised an all-encompassing system for understanding the world; both held out of the promise of a universal truth), Scholem would naturally have appreciated Dr. Renard de Montpensier's struggle with the embodiment of insanity in his rational world; with his attempts to impose rationality on the irrational; and in the kinds of questions he asked himself: "Insanity had taught the lost souls down below in the garden to dance. How would reason affect them?"

And how could a mathematics student immersed in the study of Kabbalah have resisted de Montpensier's thought that perhaps those who believed in reason and those who had lost it were "like two brothers who travel different paths to the same destination and catch sight of one another from a distance. . . . Is there no difference? Is reason only disciplined insanity, an insane hallucination that has taken on form, and under whose influence we all live? Is reason a dream created by chance, made usable by necessity?"

Benjamin seems to have left no explicit record of his thoughts about *Kzradock*, but Scholem's journals suggest that some of Levy's ideas stayed with him. On 17 June 1918, Scholem wrote that Benjamin had read to him from notes he had written (which have not survived) on dreams and clairvoyance. The note on clairvoyance included what Benjamin called "the law of the ghostly: If a being (which is always androgynous) is lost there appears, in a parallel process, a double which is the female self. The double which cannot be drawn into a unity is the sign of the ghostly."[7] In the last chapter of *Kzradock* de Montpensier writes, "The locked-away soul fashions, within itself, its own opposite. If it is a man's soul, it will produce his female opposite." With a shift to the androgynous, this is the same "law."

NOTES

1. One of Levy's poems, in a terribly corrupted form, did later receive some international recognition. In a 1938 book professing to detail a Jewish conspiracy against Germany, the poem "Der brennende Dornbusch" ("The Burning Bush") was "deciphered," as including such "secret" statements as "The Jew lives by the lie / And dies by the truth." These vile "decipherments" were being repeated as late as the 1960s by, among others, the prominent anti-Semite Benjamin Freedman.

2. Scholem to Werner Kraft, in a letter dated 14 July 1917. *A Life in Letters, 1914–1982*, ed. Anthony David Skinner (Cambridge, MA: Harvard University Press, 2002), p. 47.

3. Gershom Scholem, *Tagebücher 1917–1923*, ed. Karlfried Gründer, Herbert Kopp-Oberstebrink, and Friedrich Niewöhner (Frankfurt am Main: Suhrkamp Verlag, 2000), 178–179. My translation.

4. The word Scholem uses here, *Rechtsphilosophie*, translates as "philosophy of law," but the concerns of the entry clearly suggest that he had "moral law" in mind.

5. *Tagebücher*, 353–354. My translation.

6. *Walter Benjamin: The Story of a Friendship*, trans. Harry Zohn (New York: New York Review Books, 2003), 58.

7. *Tagebücher*, 238. My translation.

W. C. Bamberger has translated works by Gershom Scholem, Mynona, Paul Scheerbart, and Argentine-German composer Mauricio Kagel, among others. His most recent novel, *A Light Like Ida Lupino*, appeared in 2014.